CW00694086

# Smashing The Mask

## And Other Stories

Jan Baynham

# Smashing The Mask
# And Other Stories

Jan Baynham

Edited by Black Pear Press

First published in October 2019 by Black Pear Press
www.blackpear.net

Copyright © Jan Baynham
All rights reserved.

No part of this publication may be reproduced, copied, stored in
a retrieval system, or transmitted in any form or by any means
without prior permission in writing from the copyright holder.
Nor may it be otherwise circulated in any form or binding or
cover other than the one in which it is published and without
conditions including this condition being imposed on subsequent
purchasers.

All the characters in this publication, other than those clearly in
the public domain, are fictitious and any resemblance to real
persons, living or dead, is purely coincidental.

ISBN 978-1-910322-99-4

Cover design by Black Pear Press

**Black Pear Press**

# Contents

# Dedication

For Mum, with love.

# Smashing The Mask

'Haven't you forgotten something?'

Uncertain, I looked at the girl staring at me from the mirror above the narrow hall table. She had grey puffy shadows under her eyes. Exhaustion and lack-of-sleep shadows, I thought, recognising them so well.

'It's here on the table where you left it last night.'

I did what I was told. I always did what I was told, didn't I? I picked up my metaphorical mask and pulled it down over my face.

'That's better,' she said.

From behind it, I saw that her face had softened, her mouth no longer a hard, taut line and her shoulders were less hunched.

I smiled back at her. 'All ready to face the world again.'

'Not quite.' She sounded concerned. 'Your scarf's slipped. Tighten it a bit and pull it up at the back.'

It was the first time I'd had to wear it.

I looked down at the soft indigo-violet fabric that was shot with black and gold and pulled it tighter round my neck as she'd told me. She hadn't seen, had she? I'd chosen it with such care. They'd always been my favourite colours but not anymore. Those hues of purple were echoed, too, in the other mask, the souvenir porcelain one, displayed in the centre of the table. I ran my hands over the silky smooth surface and tears pricked at my eyes. I thought wistfully of our

1

honeymoon in Venice and how good life had been then. We'd ambled along the crowded narrow streets, admiring the intricate balconies and colourful frescoes on the buildings lining the canals. We'd stopped on the stone bridges to watch dark-haired men skilfully steer their gondolas along the teal-green waterways below us.

I checked that my cuffs were well down over my wrists. Mum was looking down at me from her gilded framed photo behind the girl in the mirror and I remembered her advice. I'd forgotten something else.

'Never leave the house without some colour on your lips, my girl.'

I applied a touch of blush pink lipstick to accentuate my smile. The beaming smile I was famous for. No one would ever guess.

'Happy now?'

Amy was waiting for me in the coffee bar. She'd managed to steal a few hours from her busy life with two-year-old twins, live-in mother-in-law and husband working away. She rose from her seat and kissed my cheek.

'Fran, how are you? It's been ages.'

My lips formed the smile that I'd practised in front of the girl in the mirror.

'Hi, Amy. How are the kids?' I wanted to steer the conversation away from me. It should have been so easy to confide in my best friend. After last night, I knew it was the right thing to do but what would she think of me?

'Oh, they're fine, thanks. Growing up fast. Anyway, tell me. How is that gorgeous hubby of yours?' Amy grinned. 'Still charming the pants off everyone?'

I pulled on the ends of my scarf and felt the material tighten around my neck. My insides flipped and my heart began racing. It had done this for a different reason when Amy had first introduced us. Max was good-looking and attractive, a friend of hers from work, and we were both single. We'd hit it off immediately and he made me feel so special, as if I was always the only girl in the room. It had been a long time since anyone had paid me such attention and within weeks we were a couple.

But that had all changed, hadn't it? My thoughts were interrupted. I could feel Amy's gaze settle on my eyes and she seemed to look right inside. I felt myself reddening, knowing that I couldn't put her off with white lies about how wonderful life was.

'Oh, he's fine.' I tried to keep my voice steady. The disguise was threatening to loosen and I was afraid Amy would ask more questions. 'Shall we order? I can't be too long.'

Amy didn't answer but kept looking straight at me. I squirmed.

'What? I haven't got two heads, have I?'

'Oh, it's nothing. You just seem different somehow,' she said. I looked away and fiddled with my scarf again, pulling it up at the back of my neck.

Amy stretched across the table and placed her hand on my arm. I winced.

'Right. You can cut the bullshit, Fran. What the hell has happened to you?'

My heart thudded in my chest but I pulled my mask tight. I was desperate to tell yet dared not utter a word about what was really bothering me.

'I-I-I don't know what you mean. Just a bug of some sort.'

Amy didn't take her eyes off me.

'I know you, Fran. Something's wrong, really wrong. I'm not going to be fobbed off with some old chestnut about having a bug. Your eyes give it away— they're so sad. Come on, spill.'

I knew Amy wouldn't give up. I told her how Max had changed, how, little by little, the real me had been eroded. The silent treatment when things didn't go his way. The vitriol in the words when I disagreed with him. The aggressive body language and the tantrums. All had contributed to making me feel worthless, I could see that now. He was controlling me and I didn't have the strength to fight it.

'There you know it all now,' I said, sitting back in my seat.

'Oh, Fran! Not Max. I had no idea.'

She patted my wrist and I flinched. Puzzled, she rolled back my cuff revealing violet black bruises that matched my scarf. Amy gasped and I pulled my hand away.

'He did that? The monster! Fran, you've got to get away.'

With that, Amy's mobile rang. Her face blanched as she listened.

'OK, I'll be there as soon as I can. I'll meet you at A&E,' she said. 'MiL,' she mouthed at me, pointing to her phone. Her mother-in-law was looking after the boys.

'Harry's fallen and cut himself. Badly. So sorry, Fran. I have to go now but you've got to get out, leave him. Today. I mean it. Ring me and I'll come and get you.'

Amy grabbed her coat and dashed out of the café.

'Let me know how Harry is,' I shouted after her.

I sat back down at the empty table and thought about what my best friend had said. Amy was right about me being different. He'd seen to that. I smiled as I remembered some of the silly things I'd got up to with her, like wearing as many outrageous shades of lippy as we could or trying to outdo each other by the number of pairs of shoes we owned. Fun memories were soon intruded by a vision of Max's sullen face when he'd made me take my latest pair back last week. I still can't believe I did.

I settled the bill and walked out with my head held high. Did I have the courage to do what Amy said? Something had to be done, I knew that, and I was the only one to do it. What had happened the previous evening was the first and last time. I needed to get home before him.

The black Audi was parked in the drive and I knew he wouldn't be happy coming home to an empty house. My insides tightened and my skin prickled, knowing what to expect. I let myself into the hallway as silently as I could.

'He's not happy at all. He slammed his car keys down and I can hear him crashing about in the kitchen,' the girl in the mirror said, her voice monotone, as I went to unpeel my public face. 'You'd better keep it on.' The taut mouth was back.

I looked at the Venetian mask beneath the mirror and sighed. How ironic it seemed that we'd stopped at practically every shop selling masks admiring the variety of beautiful colours and jewels. Exquisite and made of fine porcelain, it had a deep violet, almost indigo, sheen and around the edges were tiny gold lustre beads. From the left eye, there dropped a single black painted tear. The mask still took pride of place in the entrance to our home, standing as a reminder of such a happy time when Max had not yet let his mask slip even a fraction and when I had no reason to ever imagine the need to wear one. How I wished I could turn back the clock to those days.

'No, I've decided. No more mask. And no more scarf.'

The girl in the mirror gasped as I unwound the

scarf I'd used as camouflage, revealing weals of purple and black around my neck. The skin at the edges was turning to pale gold. Even Amy hadn't seen that. I felt ashamed and quickly covered the evidence with my hands. Behind the girl, Mum looked down in horror. I'd always told myself I would never be like her, always giving in, always keeping the peace, but this was worse, far worse. It was what had finally made me make up my mind to leave him. Wasn't that what Amy had said? There would be no going back to how it used to be. I knew that. He wouldn't change.

The girl in the mirror agreed. She stood up tall, lifted her eyes and held up an open palm for me to high-five.

'You can do it, Fran. You're worth so much more than this.'

Behind her, my mother was smiling in agreement and pride. I took down her photo and hugged it to my chest.

I tiptoed up the stairs and carefully pulled down an overnight suitcase from the top of the wardrobe. As well as the photo, I forced as many clothes as I could into it, rushed to the bathroom to gather toiletries and my toothbrush, I crept downstairs step by step. I had just reached the hallway when the sitting room door burst open.

'I thought I heard someone. Where the bloody hell have you been?' Max's voice boomed. He looked from me to the suitcase in my hand. 'Why, you little bitch!'

He lunged towards me and raised his fist. I dodged out of the way and he fell heavily against the hall table, losing his balance. The Venetian mask toppled and fell onto the parquet floor, shattering into shards of purple porcelain. One larger piece that held the black teardrop landed at my feet. Picking it up, I too began to shed a tear for what might have been but I had to act quickly if I was to escape. There was no time to waste.

Before Max could get to his feet, I seized the suitcase and without a backward glance, hurried away from the house. The masquerade was over.

# Burning Our Sardine

'What? One teensy, weensy sardine?' Mia said when we told her about the ceremony we were going to see at the end of the carnival.

Her mother looked at her, then me and started laughing. I felt a lump rise into my throat. It was good to hear Lucy's laugh again. It was the laugh I'd heard so much when we'd first met and the laugh that had been absent since it happened.

'It's not a real sardine, sweetheart. It's quite big, isn't it, Daddy? It's made of coloured foil and tissue paper and once it gets dark tonight it will be carried through the streets before it's burned.'

'It's said to bring good luck to the fishermen and they'll catch plenty of fish,' I said. 'Not that there are many fishermen living here any more.'

'I read that it means putting the past behind you and starting afresh.' Lucy looked straight at me. 'And then there'll be fireworks.' She tucked a stray strand of hair behind her ear and ran a finger along her scar.

Mia clapped her hands.

Perhaps the holiday would work after all. There was a visible change in the way Lucy held herself already. Her shoulders were less hunched, there was a hint of a sparkle back in her eyes and she seemed more relaxed around Mia.

*

We traipsed out of the hotel to take our place along the carnival route in plenty of time for the five o'clock start. Mia was tall for seven but we wanted her to get a good view. We decided on a spot opposite the tree-lined square in front of the tiny whitewashed church. The day before, it had been a quiet spot with just a few holidaymakers sitting at the gingham clothed tables taking coffee in the shade of the palm trees but today it thronged with hoards of visitors who had arrived for the spectacle.

'Dad. How much longer?' Mia asked.

'If you listen hard, you can hear the whistles and the drums in the distance.' I placed her on my shoulders and pointed out the flashes of colour that were visible as the procession wound its way down the hill from the top of the village, disappearing behind a row of terracotta roofs only to re-emerge into the sunshine a whole street lower down the hill.

'They're going to be ages yet,' said Lucy. 'I think I'm going to have a wander around the shops. Coming, Mia?'

'No. I'll stay with Daddy.' I saw the hurt on Lucy's face as Mia chose yet again not to spend time alone with her. I hope that's going to change over the next few days, I thought. I knew it would take time but we had to move on as a family.

I turned and watched my wife push through the crowds that were milling around the edges of the pavement. For no reason that I could think of, I clenched my hands tighter round Mia's ankles and a shiver cooled my body even though the sun was still strong. It was a fleeting feeling; a foreboding that something wasn't right but I dismissed it. I put Mia down on the pavement.

'I can't see. I want to go to the front.'

'All right. Say "Excuse me" as you move through and stay exactly where I can see you.'

By now, it was three deep along the pavement edge but I shifted to make sure Mia was in my view. She turned back to me, beaming.

'They're coming. I can see the dancers.'

The procession turned the corner by the hotel and made its way along the street where we were waiting. Colourful figures dressed in fancy dress, outrageous clowns, children from dancing troupes, men in white suits, all interacted with the crowd as they passed and the whole atmosphere was one of celebration and happiness. The visitors showed their appreciation with clapping and cheering. One strikingly beautiful dancer dressed head to toe in bright turquoise moved to our side of the street and made eye contact with me. The sequins on her leotard glinted in the bright sunshine and accentuated the curves on her slim but shapely body. Huge aquamarine feathers plumed her head and shoulders, forming wings. I smiled back at her as she moved her neck and arms as if she was a bird performing a dancing ritual to attract a mate.

'I'm back. Where's Mia?' Lucy's concerned voice

brought me back to the present.

'She's watching from the front,' I said, looking to the place where our daughter had been standing moments before. I went cold. Goose bumps formed along my neck as I realised she'd gone. I pushed through to the front and shouted for her.

'You were supposed to be looking after her,' Lucy screamed and her face blanched. She began to sob and shake.

The noise around us seemed louder, the whistles more shrill and the drums more angry.

'Have you seen a little girl? Blonde hair. About this high. She's seven.'

I knew by the look on the people's faces they didn't understand what I was saying and they moved to see past me, not to miss the spectacle of the dancing.

At that moment, everything changed. Bile rose into my throat. I didn't know which way to turn. I began running back and forth along where people had gathered. I'd never find her in that crowd. I knew I should go back to Lucy but I had to find Mia. Irrational thoughts filled my head. What if she'd been taken? What if she'd wandered off and got lost? If she'd followed the procession she could be down by the harbour by now. What if she'd fallen in?

'Whatever's wrong, mate?' It was one of the guests from the hotel. 'I saw you running through the procession. Has something happened?'

He took my elbow and guided me onto a space on

the church square.

'It's my little girl. Mia. She's gone. One minute she was there. Then she'd disappeared.' I started to shake unable to stop myself.

'Look you stay here in case she comes back. I'll go back to the hotel and get them to contact the police.'

'No. My wife. She's frantic. I have to go to her. She's over there where Mia was standing.' I pointed across the street.

'OK. You go back to her and stay put. I'll come back once I've alerted the authorities. What was she wearing, your little girl?'

My mind went blank. God, I was useless. Lucy would know. 'A turquoise printed tee-shirt, I think. Oh, and shorts. Yes, white shorts.'

Guilt flooded my mind; the same turquoise I recalled as the dancer's leotard which clung so tightly. If only I hadn't been distracted.

'I'll be back to help you search for Mia as soon as I can.' And he was gone. I didn't even know his name.

I made my way through the procession to get to Lucy. A laughing clown barred my way blowing a whistle hard in my face. Another took my hands and twirled me around. I swore at him to get off me. I caught sight of Lucy standing on tiptoe trying to see me, her face searching to see whether Mia was with me. When I got into her full view, she started to scream and came up to me, hammering my chest.

'Where is she? You've been gone for so long.

Where is she? You've lost my baby. How could you?'
Her voice was shrill, strident, and even above the din
of the carnival people were turning to watch her
distress.

Seeing Lucy like this brought it all back. The
haunted look on her face, the empty eyes blaming me.
She screamed, 'Not again. I can't bear it.' She fell to
her knees, wrapping her arms around her thin body
and rocked back and forth. I helped her up and held
her tight, so that I felt every sob.

'Sshh, my love. We'll find her. She can't have gone
far.'

Soothing words for Lucy's sake. My insides
churned. They were far from what I was really
thinking.

I saw the hotel guest coming towards us with a
young woman in tow. Even though I didn't know
them, I felt a strange sense of relief that they were
going to help us.

'The hotel manager's rung the police and they're
putting out an alert for Mia. My girlfriend will stay
with your wife if you'd like me to help you search.'

I felt sick to the pit of my stomach and just nodded
my thanks.

'Let's split and cover each side of the street and
follow the procession down to the harbour,' he said.

'OK. I'll cross over and see you down there.' My
insides flipped again and visions of Mia's long blonde
hair flowing out behind her tiny body in the water

flooded into my mind. I have to get a grip. This isn't helping anyone. I was trying to imagine where she might have gone if she had just wandered off. I darted in and out of the souvenir shops that she loved, their garish goods glowing at odds with the monochrome of my panic. She wasn't in any of them. I looked in the cafes, round corners, ran up dead-end streets and asked if anyone had seen my little girl. All the time, I was shouting her name. Everyone looked at me but no one helped.

My thoughts returned to the harbour where we'd been the day before. Mia had shown a great interest in the boats in the harbour and looked down at the water searching for the shoals of fish. She could have gone down there again and fallen in. I found myself running down the hill, pushing anyone who got in my way and catching up with the tail end of the carnival procession. I had to pull myself together and focus. Losing it wouldn't help me find her. I slowed to a brisk walk and reached the harbour wall.

'Daddy!'

I could barely breathe. I looked at the direction of the voice I knew so well and saw Mia walking hand in hand with the man who was helping me. I became lightheaded and I had to steady myself against the wall of one of the cafes. We began running towards each other and I scooped her up into my arms, unable to say anything until my sobs had subsided. Relief washed over me and the golden yellow of Mia's blonde hair together with the turquoise of her tee-shirt replaced the monochrome.

'She was walking along with the procession. Said a little girl had told her to join them.'

I put Mia down and grabbed the man's hand, shaking it for what seemed an age. 'I can't thank you enough, mate. I just went to pieces. Was imagining all sorts.'

'No worries. I'll get back to the hotel and tell them she's safe. Bye, Mia.'

I looked down at my daughter unable to believe that she was unharmed. There would be time for questions later.

We ran up the hill from the harbour. It was quieter now. The procession had passed and dusk was falling to form long shadows of the trees and buildings across the street. As we turned the corner, a lone figure with her arms outstretched was running towards us.

'Mia. Thank God.' Lucy's face crumpled as she enveloped Mia, and her whole body convulsed into sobs. I put my arms around my wife and my daughter and the three of us just stood fixed to the spot for several minutes. 'What happened? Did anyone take you? Haven't we always told you to stay near us? Why did you go off, Mia?' The panic in Lucy's voice had returned as she stood back and demanded answers. Mia moved away from her and grabbed my hand.

'Look, let's go back to the room. There's plenty of

time for questions then. The main thing is you're safe and sound, aren't you, Mia?' I picked her up and placed an arm around Lucy.

Back at the hotel, Mia was soon engrossed playing with her toys and I broached the subject again.

'The man said you joined the procession with a little girl.'

'Yes, it was Olivia.'

My heartbeat quickened and I looked at Lucy. She gasped, clamping her hand over her mouth, and her eyes filled with tears

'But, you know, it wasn't Olivia, sweetheart. Olivia died, didn't she?' I tried to sound calm.

'I know, but she said she missed having a little sister around and I was to follow her.' All the time, Mia never looked up. 'So I did,' she said, folding her arms.

It was then I realised that Lucy and I had been so wrapped up in our own grief, so worried about Lucy's recovery from the accident, that perhaps we hadn't realised that the person who'd been most affected was little Mia. Mia was the one who was waiting for her mummy and big sister to pick her up from her friend's house and couldn't understand why she'd had to stay the night without any real explanation. Telling her the following day that Olivia was dead and that Lucy was fighting for her life had been the hardest thing I'd ever had to do but what about Mia receiving the news? I don't think we'd dealt with the enormity of what it had done to our other little girl.

'I expect you miss Olivia as a big sister, too,' I said, looking over to Lucy to gauge her reaction.

'Oh, yes, we don't even talk about her, do we?'

It was true. Lucy got so upset whenever Olivia's name was mentioned.

'I told her I miss not having her to play with me as you and mummy are always so sad. She said it will get better though and I had to be a good girl.'

Lucy stifled a sob but pulled Mia in close. 'I promise you, sweetheart, we'll make some happy times for you. Like Olivia says, it will get better. I promise.'

'Starting right now,' I said.

I had a good feeling that something positive would come out of what had happened. As awful as losing Mia was for those few hours, it had brought us to our senses. We'd never forget the past, but the three of us could start afresh.

'Let's go and burn this sardine, then,' said Lucy, her eyes glistening.

# Rock-a-Bye Baby

Ali put down the roller into the tray of creamy vanilla white paint and straightened her aching back.

'There, Bubs, all done. Just the alphabet frieze to go on now and you can make an appearance any time,' she said, patting her swollen stomach. And that can't be soon enough for me.

She stood back and admired her handiwork. The baby's bedroom had been her project. It was now light and fresh, so different from the dated décor of the dingy bedroom they'd inherited. With Ben's help, she'd even stripped the floorboards back to the original pine and waxed them lovingly to a silky gleam. She and Ben had fallen in love with Rock Cottage when they came to the village searching out a prospective family home two years ago. It had been built about a hundred years ago, according to the estate agent. The history that they'd asked for was all there. The nooks and crannies, the secret passageway they'd found, the open fireplaces, all added to a character that their modern flat in London had lacked. So why did she feel uneasy?

'Ben, you can bring it up now if you like,' Ali shouted down the stairs to her husband. 'I've finished.'

Hanging the curtains and putting all the furniture in will make it feel like a baby's room, she thought. I'm just exhausted. That's it.

Minutes later, he appeared at the door with the rocking chair. Now that he'd removed all the chipped brown paint, it matched the wood of the floor.

'I can't believe the previous owners left this. It was tucked as far as you could go in a corner of the attic. Good as new, what do you think, Al?'

'Ben, it's lovely. I can just see myself feeding Bubs in the middle of the night, rocking back and forth.' Ali forced a smile, not wanting to worry Ben with her concerns. 'Let's call it a day.'

Later that night, Ali just couldn't get comfortable. No matter which way she lay, 'the bump' got in the way and it was taking her a long time to get to sleep. She normally went straight off as soon as her head hit the pillow but that night she tossed and turned, unable to fathom what was bothering her. She was aware of the usual rhythm of Ben's breathing, but there was something else—a faint knocking sound coming from the next room that she hadn't heard before. It became like a worm in her head. Once she was aware of it, it drowned out all other sounds in the room and she crept out of bed to investigate.

Ali lifted the latch of the door and looked into the baby's bedroom which was bathed in moonlight. Just where Ben had left it earlier, the old chair was rocking, back and forth, back and forth, as if someone had just got up from it. She looked over at the bare window and saw a young woman, holding her arms as if she was cradling a baby.

Ali slammed the door and stood for a moment

gripping the latch as if to imprison what she'd just seen in the room. Her heart was pounding.

'Ben, Ben,' she shouted. 'You've got to come.'

'What on earth's the matter?' A bleary-eyed Ben emerged from the next room. 'God, Ali, you look as if you've seen a—'

'Ghost? Well I have...in there. You look.'

Ben opened the door of the baby's bedroom and turned on the light.

'There's nothing in here apart from the old rocking chair. Come and see for yourself.'

Ali stepped in and took comfort in her husband's arms. 'No really. The rocking chair was rocking and over by the window...' She began to cry.

Putting a reassuring arm around her, Ben took her back to their room. 'I think you've just got over tired and your imagination's got the better of you, Al.'

It makes sense, she thought. I have been overdoing it. Ben's right. She put all thoughts about the young woman and the rocking chair out of her mind and drifted off to sleep.

It was two weeks later when Ali thought about that night again. By then, the frieze was decorating the uneven walls of the baby's bedroom, the matching curtains were gracing the window and nursery furniture was all in place. The rocking chair stood motionless under the eaves.

'I still can't believe how stupid I was, Bubs,' she

said aloud. 'Won't be long now, will it?'

She closed the door behind her and as she did so, she heard 'Rock-a-Bye Baby' being sung, very softly. She re-opened the door and saw that the rocking chair was rocking in time to the lullaby. The young woman whom she'd seen previously was sitting cradling an invisible baby and looking lovingly down as she sang. When she saw Ali, she disappeared into a silvery mist taking her singing with her but leaving behind an empty chair which rocked itself to a stand-still. Ali stood fixed to the spot not quite understanding what she had just seen.

So I wasn't imagining things, Ben, she thought. That's twice now. Who can she be? Why is there no baby? Why didn't I see her before? We've lived here for two years, for Pete's sake.

With all these thoughts whizzing round in her head, Ali realised that whereas she'd been terrified the first time she'd seen her, this time she was completely calm. There was something lovely about the way the young woman looked at the baby that wasn't there. Almost maternal.

'She looked sad too,' she told Ben that evening. 'And her clothes. The floral dress and pearl-buttoned cardigan reminded me of photos of Gran taken during the war. Her hairstyle was the same as well. You know the way they used to roll the ends up.'

'Ali, just think about what you're saying. You really want me to think you've seen a ghost, a real ghost.

Remember, you told the estate agents you didn't believe in them when he asked if you minded being shown any haunted properties.'

'I know but I hadn't seen a real one then and she's completely harmless.'

When Ben left for work the next morning, Ali set to work too. She was going to find out everything she could about who had lived in the house before, especially anyone living there about the time of WWII. Her best bet was the Post Office. The postmistress knew everything that went on. Ali waited until the queue had gone and the shop was empty.

'Hello, Mrs Thomas. You've lived in the village all your life, haven't you? I'm trying to find out all about Rock Cottage. It seems a shame that all Ben and I know about it is what the estate agent told us. She said the previous owners never really settled but couldn't say why.'

The elderly postmistress came round to the front of the counter. 'I'd be delighted to, dear. But I've only got what my old Mum told me, mind but she was a bit of a hoarder. She said all the children in the village used to call it "Rock-a-Bye Baby" Cottage when I was a little girl.'

Ali smiled. I can imagine, she thought. Why is Mrs Thomas giving me that searching look?

'It's half day tomorrow, dear. Why don't you come over for a cup of tea and I'll dig out a few of my mother's photos and I'll tell you what I can about the Rock?'

Ali busied herself all the next morning while waiting until she could visit Mrs Thomas. Just as she was about to put on her coat, she heard it again:

Rock-a-bye baby on the tree top
When the wind blows, the cradle will rock
When the bough breaks, the cradle will fall
And down will come baby, cradle and all.

Who was the young woman? Would Mrs Thomas have the answers Ali was looking for?

'Come in, dear. I've put the kettle on. You have a look through these and see if there's anything to interest you,' said Mrs Thomas, taking Ali's coat. 'Milk and sugar?'

'Just milk, thanks, Mrs Thomas. Wow, you've got some stuff here.'

She looked at the piles of photos and a letter in front of her. Ali looked at the pile that had been sorted into date order first. Mrs Thomas's mother had been one of those who wrote the date on the back of each photo.

'This is wonderful,' she said. 'Do you think any of these people in the photos may have lived at Rock Cottage before us?'

Mrs Thomas placed a tray of the two cups of tea

and a plate of chocolate biscuits down on the coffee table. 'Help yourself, dear. Yes, see these here. I picked them out last night.'

She laid out three photos in front of Ali. 'This is dated 1937 and Mum would have been about sixteen. Next to her is her friend, Mabel, who's the same age. Here they are in this one swimming down at Black Bridge dated 1939 and in this one in 1942, Mum is bridesmaid at Mabel's wedding.' She looked up from the photos. 'Are you all right? You look a bit peaky?'

Ali fixed her gaze at one of the young women in the photos, the same one who sang lullabies and rocked an invisible baby in her cottage. But there was one big difference. Here, she looked happy, full of love, a new bride gazing into the face of a handsome airman so different from the sad, wistful soul that occupied Rock Cottage now.

'Do you know any more about Mabel?' Ali asked. 'Did she and your mum stay friends?'

'Oh yes, dear. Such a tragic turn of events. She was expecting almost straight away, a honeymoon baby Mum said, but her husband Colin was posted overseas and never saw the baby. He was shot down over France the following month. Mum was with her when she got the telegram. She was in a right old state, Mum said. It was just her and the baby, then. A little boy; she called him Colin after his dad. But life's so cruel isn't it?'

Ali nodded thinking of the gaunt look on Mabel's

face now. But why was there no baby Colin in her arms each time she'd seen her?

'Poor girl. That wasn't the end of it. The baby...' Mrs Thomas clasped her hand over her lips as if to stop the words coming out.

'Go on, what were you going to say about the baby?' Ali insisted.

'That'll be a story for another time,' the old lady said, trying to change the subject.

'You've started now. Please tell me. I'm imagining all sorts of terrible things.'

'The baby died too when it was six weeks old. Sudden death I think we'd call it now...Oh I'm so sorry, my dear, me and my big mouth. I shouldn't have said what with you so close to you having yours.'

Tears were streaming down Ali's face. 'That's so sad. But, no, Mrs Thomas, that's not why I'm upset.'

She then told the old lady exactly what was happening at Rock Cottage and wondered if she'd think her as potty as Ben did.

Mrs Thomas reached across and patted her hand. 'Don't worry, Alison. It's just lovely that Mabel has at last got a friend, a fellow mum-to-be, living in her house. You mark my words. Mabel will be gone once that beautiful baby of yours arrives.'

Ali looked puzzled and waited for Mrs Thomas to explain.

'After baby Colin died, Mabel became a bit of a recluse. She wouldn't even let my mother in to see her.

Mum said as she got close to the front door she would sometimes hear Mabel singing "Rock-a-Bye Baby". It was her favourite lullaby to get baby Colin off to sleep. Before he died, she'd sit in her rocking chair singing it to the baby so I suppose she just carried on.'

It all fits, Ali thought. But why did Mrs Thomas say it would all end soon?

'So you see now why all us children used to call it "Rock-a-Bye Baby" cottage. She lived alone like that just having groceries and milk delivered, leaving money to pay the bills under a flat stone by the front step and not bothering with anyone until she died about ten years later. She was still a young woman. Died of a broken heart, Mum said. Colin would have been about my age now.'

'So why do you think she'll go when I have the baby?' Ali asked.

'Because of this.' Mrs Thomas handed her a letter. 'She wrote it to Mum. They found it on the hall table after she died.'

The paper was crumpled and the ink faded but one sentence jumped out at Ali.

'There will be a new baby in the cottage one day and until there is, I'll stay waiting and guarding until his arrival.'

'So you see, my dear. Mabel's been waiting for you and that lovely young husband of yours to bring a new baby to Rock Cottage. It lay empty for years after she died. Then, the first sale was to a property developer who ripped all the character out of the place. The next people spent years putting it all back in again and used it as a weekend second home. So you see why I'm so excited to see you and Ben turn it into a family home just like Mabel wanted.'

'Why didn't you warn me about Mabel, then? I was so scared that first time,' Ali said.

'I wasn't sure if she'd reveal herself to you. The last couple didn't say they'd seen her. They just said the back room always felt as if there was a cold spot...next to the radiator of all places. They didn't stay long. When they said their dogs were their babies, I knew she'd still hang around.'

Ali got up to go and a sharp pain seared through her. 'I think I'd better be getting back. And thank you. I shan't worry now if I hear haunting lullabies and rocking chairs.'

Ali sat up in her hospital bed, looking over at the cradle of her new born son.

'What do you think of Colin for a middle name, after your Dad?' she asked Ben before he had a chance to sit down.

'Oh, Mrs Thomas left this for Oliver. I didn't know you'd been over to see her yesterday. Colin? Oliver Colin; mmm, that has a nice ring to it. Yes, I think he'll be delighted.'

And so will Mabel.

She unwrapped the present from Mrs Thomas. It

was a musical mobile for baby Oliver's cot. She turned the knob and held it by the sleeping baby's crib.

Rock-a-bye baby on the tree top
When the wind blows, the cradle will rock
When the bough breaks, the cradle will fall
And down will come baby, cradle and all.

Ali gasped and placed her hand over her mouth. You'll be able to rest in peace now, Mabel, she thought. Unless you want to stay and watch over Oliver Colin for us, of course?

*First published by Alfie Dog Fiction (2014)*

# Missing Without Trace

'Idiot! Just cut me up, why don't you?' Mark thumped the horn and kept his hand there. 'Did you see that?'

It was impossible not to as Mark swerved our car to the left. I gripped the edge of my seat and tasted bile rising to my mouth.

'Stop, Mark, please. I'm going to be sick.'

He signalled and pulled over allowing the stream of cars to pass just in time for me to make a dash for the grass verge. I heaved and retched, not able to stop shaking.

'What ever is it, Lizzie? You look dreadful. Sorry if I scared you, love.'

Clammy beads of perspiration formed on my forehead. Deeply buried memories of a blue and white car that I didn't understand flooded my mind. Mark's voice was fuzzy in the distance.

'Blokes like that make me so mad. He'd have hit us if I'd not swerved.'

'It's not you, Mark. I'll be all right. Come on, let's get home.'

My hand went subconsciously to the right side of my head, seeking out the spot where I felt an intense searing pain. It throbbed for just a fleeting moment and then disappeared.

I tried to push the lingering uneasy feeling to the back of my mind. We took our usual route so why was I straining my neck at every little cove we passed?

What was I looking for?

'Home at last,' Mark said, as he pulled the car into the gravel lane alongside the cottage. 'I'm so glad we decided to move down here, aren't you, Lizzie? Beats city life any day.'

I agreed and relaxed as we unpacked the car and entered the house.


The first thing I noticed when I woke screaming was the smell. It was the newness of the leather seats in the car. The pain on the right side of my head was back.

'It's OK, love. You're safe. Here, sip this.' Mark handed me a glass of water. 'You haven't had a nightmare for ages, have you? Certainly not down here at the cottage. I wonder what brought that on.'

I could feel tears pricking behind my eyelids. I remembered times at our London flat I'd woken to find him coaxing me to drink some cool water and his voice soothing me to breathe slowly and deeply until the panic subsided. Doctors put it down to stress at work.

'I think I know,' I said, hesitating. 'Promise you'll hear me out?' I waited until he nodded. 'You know that car that cut us up today?'

'That old blue and white one?'

'Yes. Well, I've been in that when it was brand new. It had tan leather seats, I remember. He was so proud of it. His first new car.' Of course. That's why I'd reacted the way I had! More was coming back to me. I

31

knew from Mark's open mouth that this was not going to be easy.

'You do know that car was brand new about fifty odd years ago? Twenty years before you were born.'

'Yes, I remember the year. 1962. "Brand new car, brand new model", he said.'

'Lizzie, you're not making any sense. Who is the he you're talking about?'

I started to cry. 'His name was Tony Carter. He offered me a ride in his new car. We went to the beach. Just for a swim, I said, but he had other ideas.'

Mark took my hands and looked straight at me. 'You have to get it into your head that it's a nightmare. It didn't really happen, Lizzie.'

'But it did. I think I was murdered in a past life. No, I don't think, I know. Tony Carter murdered me. I'm one of those missing people that you read about. Missing without trace. Please, Mark, please. You have to help me.'

Mark raised his hands in the air, unable to understand and at a loss to know what to say to me. He got back into bed.

'Let's try and get some sleep. We'll talk about it in the morning,' he said, brushing his lips on my cheek. It was always his way of dealing with things.

I reluctantly agreed, filled with a sense of dread of the hours that were left before daylight. Every time I closed my eyes, the image of a sheltered cove came into focus and my eyes rested on the rocks where we stood and I looked out to sea. The pain intensified in my head, on the right side, and tears fell in silence onto my pillow.

The next morning, I found Mark at his laptop.

'What are you looking for?' I knew it would be something to do with my nightmare the night before.

He didn't answer at first but then said, 'I didn't sleep a wink last night, going over and over what you told me. Your reaction frightened me, Lizzie. You really believe you were there in that car and that Tony fella murdered you, don't you?'

At last. 'We have to find the cove, Mark. I'm sure it's along the road we always use to get here. No one has found my remains yet.'

'Look at this. There are doctors who can take patients right back in their memory.' He pointed to the screen. He had to force himself to add, 'Even into a past life.'

As I read some of the stories, I began to feel that I wasn't alone.

Mark interrupted my thoughts. 'It's worth a try, love. But first I think we need to contact the police to see if there were any young girls reported missing in 1962.'

'Mr and Mrs Thompson, please come in and sit down,' said the detective inspector. We were ushered into the interview room and he indicated two chairs on the opposite side of the desk. 'I'm DI Morris and this is my colleague, DC Jackie Peters.'

I smiled at them both.

'Now, I have to be honest with you, Mrs Thompson, when we first heard that you wanted to speak to us on this matter, we were very sceptical to say the least.' The DI glanced across at his female colleague. 'But, and it's only a tentative enquiry at this point, mind, we have been in touch with Missing Persons. If they can tell us that there's a young woman—aged about seventeen, you say?—who's been on their missing persons file since 1962 then we'll pursue it further.'

I could feel goose bumps pushing through the skin on my arms and an icy chill seeped from every bone in my body.

'My name was Carly then,' I said, softly. Mark searched for my hand and gave it a reassuring squeeze.

DI Morris looked again at his colleague. 'Tell us in your own words what you think happened to Carly, Mrs Thompson.'

I repeated to the police officers what I remembered. My head throbbed with increasing excruciating pain and my heart raced faster as more memories surfaced. It was so real to me but I could tell by the way they both looked at one another they were unconvinced by my story.

'Look, we can't do any more until we hear back from Missing Persons. Why don't you go home and I'll ring as soon as we have some information?' said the detective inspector when I finished speaking.

He rose to his feet and shook our hands before we left.


Later that day, the telephone rang and Mark answered.

'Really. So she was right. All right, officer, I'll tell her. Thank you.'

Mark entered the room, his face pale and drawn, and I knew that this was the start of something neither of us knew anything about before the incident with the blue and white car.

'You were right, Lizzie. A girl from the village did go missing in 1962. Exactly as you said. Seventeen years old and guess what her name was? Carly Young.'

He went on, 'Missing without trace, apparently. No body found, no one charged.'

Knots tightened in my stomach. 'So, what's next then?'

'DI Morris has arranged for you to see a specialist in past-life regression therapy. That's hypnotising you to go back through memories before you were born, even into a past life, to me and you. That way they can hopefully find out where Carly Young's body is. Are you up for it?'


'Hello, Carly. Tell me how you met Tony.'

'Used to come into Smokey Joe's, the caff where I worked. Always played the Juke Box I remember.

Played Carole King over and over. Told me it might as well rain until September if I didn't go out wiv 'im.'

'What was he like, this Tony?' the doctor asked. His manner was reassuring, coaxing me to continue.

'Thought 'e were above the other lads. 'ad money, see. Take that car of 'is. Classic Ford, 'e said it were. Brand new, what wiv 'im working at Dagen'am cars. Beautiful blue and white. I can still smell them leather seats now. Good fun, tho'. Lovely brown eyes. Long 'air, curly. He laughed a lot but you wouldn't want to cross 'im, mind. Always flirtin', tellin' me how pretty I were, how 'e weren't goin' to give up on me.'

'So did you go out with him in the end?'

'Oh, yeah, but I took some persuadin', I can tell you.'

'Where did you go?' The doctor's voice soothed me into speaking more slowly.

'Well, 'e picked me up in the lane behind the caff one Saturday. Didn't tell a soul. They'd only say 'e were too old what wiv me being only seventeen. Said we was goin' to the beach.' I shifted in my seat.

'It's all right, Carly. Take your time.'

'He parked the car by this little cove. No one else were there. We took off our shoes. Started walking along the beach towards the light'ouse. The feel of the sand between me toes were lovely, told 'im it were proper romantic. I 'eld 'is 'and like 'e told me to. Said 'e loved me and that I should show him 'ow grateful I were. Grateful for what? I said.'

36

My head was throbbing with pain. I put my hand to the exact spot where it felt as if a red hot poker was piercing my skull.

'What happened next, Carly?' The doctor spoke in gentle tones.

'"You know what", 'e said. "Takin' you out". Pulled me towards 'im, rough like. Started tuggin' at me blouse, puttin' 'is 'and in. I said, no, and 'e stopped, fair does, but I knew 'e didn't like it. We climbed on the rocks. I turned away to look at the light'ouse. It was then that 'e did it.'

Tears were streaming down my face. I jerked my head one way then the other.

'Carly, do you want to stop?' The doctor looked concerned but I had to tell him the whole story.

'"it me on the back of me 'ead, 'e did, wiv a rock.' I screamed and threw my head back against the chair.

'Carly, you don't have to say any more,' the doctor said.

'See 'ere.' I brought my head forward, pointing to the right side. In a whisper, I said, 'I must 'ave left me body then. I watched 'im stuff it into a gap in the rocks and cover it. All limp, I were. 'e threw the rock covered in blood out to sea. The water turned pink, then a wave turned it back to clear. What 'e'd done moments before all washed away, like.' I felt ice-cold, yet sweat formed on my brow at the same moment. Time seemed to be running out but the doctor told me there was no rush. I took another sip of water.

'Just turned and went, 'e did. Not even a backward glance. All them years I've been waitin', waitin' to be found.' I shuddered and sobbed uncontrollably. A voice in the distance was calling me.

'Lizzie, Lizzie. You can come back now. Journey back through time. Think of the happy little girl you were, your family. Remember Mark, how you met and think of your wedding day. Come back to the present.'

I looked down at the sodden paper tissues in my hand but inside I felt an unfamiliar, calm serenity. Something had happened in that room. I didn't know what but it bode well for the future, I was sure of it.

The phone was ringing when we arrived back at the cottage.

'All right, Inspector. I'll tell her. We've just got back now. Thanks,' Mark said. 'That was the DI. He said they've found what they think will be confirmed as Carly's body. Says it should be on the local news tonight. Quick, Lizzie, turn it on.'

We both rushed into the sitting room and sat down to watch.

'Thanks to a tip-off from a member of the public, human remains have been uncovered at Lighthouse Cove, a local beauty spot,' the newsreader said. 'A police spokesman said that a forensics team had identified them as belonging to a young female.'

Mark held my hand to steady the shaking. I fixed my gaze at the TV screen.

'This is all because of you, love.'

I felt tears trickling down my cheeks.

'Do you think they'll charge Tony Carter with her murder? Is he still alive, even?' I said.

Mark put his arm around me and kissed my forehead. 'Let's hope that he can be traced by that blue and white Classic car that cut us up. You've given the police so much to go on, Lizzie. It's up to them now.'

> NEWSFLASH—Essex man charged with the murder in 1962 of Carly Young, a seventeen-year-old girl on the Missing Persons' register. Police have named him as Anthony Carter aged 76 and he will appear before magistrates in the morning.

'You OK?' Mark asked.

I nodded. 'DI Morris said it was Carter's grandson driving like a maniac that morning. Tony Carter's a frail old man now. We're just lucky that he kept the blue and white car, I suppose.'

'Because of you, Lizzie, Carly's family will at last get closure about what happened all those years ago and Tony Carter will get what he deserves.'

I knew that there was closure for someone else at long last, too.

'Rest in peace, Carly,' I said, in a whisper.

*First published by Alfie Dog Fiction (2014)*

# The Unbroken Bond

I've been awake for most of the night, unable to believe what will be happening today. Drawing back the curtains to let in some light, I look over at Steve who's still asleep and wonder if he'll understand the mixture of feelings I have, a melee of excitement, elation, panic even. It's the day I've rehearsed in my head so many times. The love I'm feeling is surely the most enduring and powerful of all the emotions. It's a bond that is never broken no matter how much time has passed, no matter how much heartache has been felt.

'What are you doing there, love?' Steve's words interrupt my thoughts. 'You'll catch your death. Come back to bed. It's too early to get up yet.'

'In a minute,' I say, not wanting him to see I've been crying.

'Big day today, Ange. Sure you don't want me to drive you?'

'No, I'll be fine, thanks. I know where to go.'

The next few hours just drag by. I make endless cups of tea for us both. Steve doesn't comment on my fidgeting and fussing but the concerned look on his face tells me he knows. He understands and senses the turmoil of emotions I'm feeling. At last, it's time to go.

'Good luck, Ange.' Steve brushes a kiss on my cheek as I leave.

This is something I need to do on my own.

I walk up the tree-lined drive to the house. The surrounding parkland is alive with autumn colours, rich with warmth, and in such stark contrast to the monochrome deadness I'd felt when I'd left there. It's as if an invisible elastic thread, stretched yet not broken, is pulling me back over a lifetime to where I truly belong. The café is crowded when I enter and, although I have a photo, it doesn't really help. Soon, I notice a casually dressed young woman looking rather bewildered and when she makes eye contact, my stomach churns and flips over. She's far too young to be my daughter. This isn't Christine. Yet there's something familiar about her. Although many years have passed, I know those ice blue eyes anywhere. They have to be Simon's and she's blonde like him, too. She walks towards me. There's an incredibly long pause.

'Mrs Davies? Mrs Angie Davies?' she says, holding out her hand. 'I'm Laura, Pauline's daughter.'

'But…I don't understand.' I start to stammer, my heart beating hard. 'Where's Pauline? It was all arranged. Is she all right?'

'She's fine. Come on. Let's sit down. Mum chickened out at the last minute. She was all set for the big reunion. Got ready and everything. I was there helping her but all of a sudden she burst into tears and became inconsolable.'

'But why now?' I say, unable to hide my

41

disappointment.

'She says she can't risk being rejected again. She's scared, Mrs Davies, really scared. She knows you say you had no choice but she says she would never, ever have given me away and she can't understand why you did what you did.'

It's now my turn to get upset. Laura hands me a tissue and pats my arm. People around us look our way, casting furtive, stolen glances.

'You and your mother will never know what it was like back then. My father thought I was the lowest of the low. I've thought about her every single day since she was born.'

Sobbing quietly, I tell Laura my story. 'I was seventeen years old in 1967, an only child, living in a small rural village with my elderly parents. I'd just left school.'

'You're not going out in that skirt,' my dad said, complaining. 'You'll catch your death in it. It's more like a pelmet!'

'Oh, Dad, not again. You're so behind the times!'

I laughed and made for the door before he said any more. Everything was good then. I was enjoying my first job in the local solicitor's office and the independence my small salary brought me. I had plenty of friends and, above all, I was hopelessly in love for the first time. Simon, who was the son of the solicitor I worked for, had come home from university to work in the family firm for the summer.

'I can never see your parents approving of me as your girlfriend. I'm just not good enough,' I said to Simon when he first asked me out. 'Their very own temp without even an O level to her name.'

'Well what about yours?' he said, scoffing. 'Our little Angie's far too young to be going out with boys, you know.' Simon pulled me towards him. 'If only they knew what their little Angie was really like.'

We began meeting in secret and, whenever we could, we stole precious moments together.

'Secret means exciting,' Simon said, whispering in my ear. I felt as if I was walking on air. For years afterwards, I would feel myself blushing when I remembered those first kisses.

'Something's put a smile on your face.' My mum teased me. 'I bet it's got something to do with a lad!'

'I'll tell you soon enough if there's something to tell.'

Little did I know then it would not be long before I most definitely would have something to tell. My world was to come crashing down almost as soon as my happiness had started.

I discovered that Simon was very experienced as far as girls were concerned. He told me if I really loved him, I would want to show him with more than kisses. He was very persuasive.

'Look, Angie, let me be the first. You are so special.'

Why, oh why, did I believe him? How could I have been so gullible? I did agree though. I loved him so much.

'Simon, I don't seem to see much of you anymore,' I said a few days later when I eventually summoned up the courage to seek him out. 'Have I done something to upset you?'

I didn't really get an answer. Simon skirted around with vague excuses and the snatched moments dwindled to almost none. Why are those girls whispering and giggling whenever I enter the office? I asked myself. Why do they go silent when I look their way? I felt myself blushing. Surely, he hasn't told them, has he? I thought, in horror. With that, Simon entered the room. My doubts were brushed aside. Just the sight of his blond hair and blue eyes was enough to convince me he was the man for me and always would be.

It had been a particularly hot day when I fainted. I was standing by the Xerox machine when I felt dizzy and slumped onto the tiled floor. It was Simon's father, my boss, who found me and a doctor was promptly sent for.

After asking some searching questions, the doctor told me I was pregnant. I went cold and goose bumps formed along my neck.

'I can't be. My mum and dad will kill me! I'll lose my job here. How will I manage?'

'What about the baby's father?' asked the doctor.

'No, he mustn't know,' I said firmly. I decided there and then it was better if Simon did not know. I knew deep down he did not love me as much as I loved him. No, I'll do this on my own.

If his father did tell about the drama in his office that day, Simon never asked me why I'd fainted and our romance ended just as quickly as it had started. The next few weeks of turmoil altered my life forever. Telling Mum first, then Dad, had been the hardest.

'How could you, Angela? Bringing such shame on the family. Haven't your dad and me brought you up proper…?'

My mother's voice trailed off as she stifled the tears.

In contrast, my dad was stony faced and furious.

'No one must ever know. You'll just have to go away and have it. You can forget any idea of keeping it.'

Feeling so alone, not being able to tell anyone about the baby growing inside me was the worst thing. The distress I felt when I left the village to enter the home for unmarried mothers over sixty miles away stayed with me for the rest of my life. My beautiful daughter was born five months later. Looking down at that little bundle, I knew, whatever happened, the bond between us would always be there. I was totally unprepared for how much I would love her. I named her Christine.

Tears burned my eyes whenever I relived the pain of the final moment when I was made to sign my baby daughter of six weeks over to her adoptive parents.

'Sign here,' said the grim faced official.

I felt they were ripping part of me away. I threw the pen across the room.

He sighed and said with a sneer, 'Be reasonable.

What kind of life can you offer her?'

'But she's mine. I can't bear to lose her.'

I burst into tears again.

He pressed his lips together and looked at me as if I was from the gutter.

'You should have thought of that nine months ago, miss. There's only one way to solve this. If you don't sign, I shall declare you of unsound mind and you know what that means, don't you?'

The mental institution. I picked up the pen and signed. They'd won. I finally gave in, made to feel like a criminal. Surely, being naïve was all that I'd been guilty of. I'd been swayed by the charms of a handsome young man, that was all, and I'd paid the price. Some part of me closed down that day.

I never did return to live with my parents but found work in the town close to St Saviour's, the mother and baby home where I'd had my daughter. Deep down I must have felt I didn't want to leave the place which held the best and the worst of memories. I used to walk past there sometimes and imagine what might have been if only things had turned out differently, imagine what my baby girl was doing with her adoptive parents. Was she happy? I hoped she had a good life.

I hadn't expected to find love again, afraid of being hurt, I suppose. After what happened, I treated all men with suspicion. But then I met Steve. He was different and with him friendship came before romance. Such a kind man and a wonderful father to our two boys. He was twice the character Simon had been. I could see that. We married just over forty years ago and he knew all about the baby girl I had given away. We talked at length about the stigma of being an unmarried mother back then and how these days he would have adopted her when he married me if I'd only been allowed to keep her. Steve was the only person who knew how deeply it had affected me over the years. Every year on Christine's birthday, he bought me a little present and we'd drink her health. Just acknowledging she existed helped me with my loss.

'Look, love,' he said some years later. 'I think you should try to trace Christine. It's becoming more common these days and I've been thinking, even if she doesn't want to meet you, at least you will have tried. I can see it's eating you up even after all these years. It's never going to go away.'

I think I loved him even more that day.

The search began and with Steve's help my Christine was traced. It took a while and at times, I thought we'd never find her. She was called Pauline now, she told me when I contacted her. It turned out she lived just ten miles away from where we raised our own family. How sad to think of her being so close. What if I'd passed my own daughter, not knowing what she looked like? I'd missed seeing her grow up, missed all the milestones in her life but at least she'd been happy. That was all I wanted for her, the only reason I gave her up in the first place. What sort of life would she have had with me, unmarried and alone, as I thought then? Her adoptive parents were no longer alive so she didn't feel disloyal, she said. She felt ready to find out more about her birth mother and had been trying to trace me too. We arranged to meet up and I hoped it would be the start of something new for both of us.

It doesn't look as if will be, now, I thought.

'So, that's my story, Laura. You see why I chose to meet here. It seems fitting we should meet at the café which was built on the site of St Saviour's, don't you think?'

Laura is listening intently to my story and nods, wiping away a tear with the back of her hand. She pats her stomach, and for the first time, I notice a small bump under her sweater. Her eyes fill with more tears.

'I'm sure you'll be reunited with mum some day soon. She was really thrilled when she found out you were looking for her as well. And then this happened. I just think she got cold feet.'

She looks away.

'You're having a baby.' I stretch across the table and take her delicate hand in mine.

She nods.

'Mum and Dad were really upset to start but they've been brilliant. It's going to be so different for this little one.'

'Things have moved on now, my dear. I would never have given your mum up if things were like they are today. You must believe me, Laura.'

'I think that's why Mum was so hurt when I told her…History repeating itself, she said.'

I look across at the child opposite.

'That little baby will be very much loved, I'm sure.'

Laura leans across the table and hands me a coloured photograph of a middle-aged woman. 'Mum wanted you to have this. It was taken a few weeks ago.'

My insides lurch again.

'I look like her, don't I?' Laura says. 'Where do we get our blonde hair from? I don't think it's from you, is it?'

She looks closely across at my grey hair which still has enough dark to show how it once had been.

Before she asks any more questions, I say, 'Your mum is the image of her father, Simon.'

'It's not just the looks I get from him either. You say my great-grandfather was a solicitor? That's what I'm going to do,' Laura says. 'I'm studying law at Manchester—well, was. I'm having to put my degree on hold for a while. But Mum and Dad have said I must finish it and they're going to help with the baby when I transfer to a uni near home.'

With that, she rises from her seat and hands me an envelope. The handwriting with its evenly formed letters and uniform loops resembles my own.

'Mum's written you a letter. You don't need to read

it here. Wait until you're somewhere more private.' Her soft voice is comforting.

She comes over and hugs me hard. 'I've got to go. I'll tell Mum all about you,' she says with a smile. 'Don't worry. I'm sure it won't be long.' She hesitates, 'Oh, and one more thing. Can I call you Gran?'

I can only nod as the tears fall again. Trying to compose myself, I catch sight of my granddaughter leaving. I follow and walk out through the door into the frosty sunlight. I feel alone, not as wretched as I did when I left here all those years ago, but the stone I hoped would be rolled away forever this afternoon is still there. A little lighter, maybe, but still weighing down my heart. I don't blame Pauline. The bond is still intact though; my baby, my daughter. Nothing can change that. And now I've met Laura, a granddaughter I didn't know I had, and I'll soon be a great-grandmother too. I take out my phone and dial Steve's number.

'How did it go, love?' the voice at the other end says. 'I've been thinking about you.'

'Can you pick me up please, Steve?'

I clutch my precious letter in my hand, holding it tight to my chest.

*First published by Creative Frontiers (2015)*

# Rising From The Ashes

The shrill whine of a siren sent shivers of alarm through me, waking me from deep sleep. I sat up with a jolt. It was real. Close by. Grabbing my fleecy dressing gown, I ran to the bedroom window and pulled back the curtains. 'Noooooo!' I screamed.

'Sam? Whatever's wrong?'

I turned to face Andy. He threw back the duvet and rushed to my side.

'It's the school. It's on fire.'

Across the road from our schoolhouse, the Victorian building was engulfed in flames. The silhouette of wooden rafters formed black bars against the scarlet sky and billows of dense smoke trailed high above the blazing shell. Firemen darted into action and hosed the fire with jets of water.

My heart thumped against my rib cage. Tears streamed down my cheeks as I gripped the school railings. Even they felt hot in my hands. The coldest night of the year, the forecaster had said. Well not here. My precious school, the heart of this village, is disintegrating before my very eyes!

'I have to do something, Andy. Everything's in there. I can't let it all go up in flames.'

'You heard what the fire officer said, Sam. They're doing what they can. At least, the Juniors' demountable classrooms are safe. If they can control the fire in the main building, it may not be so bad.'

But they couldn't. It was hopeless. I watched, helpless and empty, as more and more crews and engines arrived. Armies of men in yellow helmets battled relentlessly against the shooting flames and intense heat. The early hours ticked away towards dawn. Red changed to dense black; all that was left was a smouldering shell and a deathly silence. A local landmark razed to the ground.

Crowds of villagers began to gather around the entrance to the school. Rumours soon circulated that three local youths had been seen fleeing the premises. Could the fire have been deliberate?

One parent came up to me, sobbing. 'Mrs Jenkins, I'm so sorry. I'm gutted. How could they? Boys from up Parry Street, so they do say.'

'We don't know that yet, Mrs Thomas,' said Andy, trying to sound calm.

Another young mum wouldn't let go of my hand as if I was an invisible link to part of her history. 'I went to your school. It's the best ever.'

'What am I going to say to Kelly? It's tragic.' Helen Jones tried hard to hold back tears.

'I'm going to see all the other parents. I'm determined. We'll ask for donations. Any money we can raise will help the children get back to school, and normality, as soon as possible.'

More parents arrived, some holding the hands of pupils, all with offers to help. The more I looked at the faces of the children, the more desolate I felt and I was grateful when Andy led me away to view the devastation of what had happened.

'Did you see their little faces? I don't know what to do. I really don't.'

'Come on. You've had a huge shock. It's better if you see it for yourself, love, and then we can start to make plans for what happens next.'

The school was just a pile of charred remains, a mesh of criss-crossed burnt embers that had fallen from the roof beams. We couldn't enter the building. It was a potential crime-scene, the policeman said. Not safe anyway. We stood as close as we could. The firemen were wading from classroom to classroom through a sludge of black ash mixed with water. It could be any building. The silence was deafening, unnatural, eerie. The heart had gone out of it. I closed my eyes and thought of the buzzing atmosphere of the little ones just like Kelly playing and learning. I heard the excited chatter of friends. I started to cry and my whole body racked with sobbing.

Andy pulls me towards him.

'Let it all out, love. You've had a terrible shock.'

'How could they, Andy? To think those yobs spent some of their happiest days with us. What happened to them to make them act like this?' I began to shake with anger.

Andy stood back to hold my shoulders firmly. He looked straight into my eyes. 'We have to show whoever did this that we won't be beaten. Right, Sam?'

I nodded through a blur of tears.

I didn't sleep much that night. Every time I closed my eyes all I could see was the building alight with scarlet and orange flames leaping like the vicious tongues of serpents into the sky. When I did drop off to sleep, I woke up bathed in perspiration worrying about how a school with no home could begin to function again. The children had to be educated and this could be the excuse the authorities needed to shut the village school with falling rolls and to bus the children elsewhere. A village without a school, that can't be right. If it was arson, those boys had destroyed more than a grey stone-built building. They'd destroyed a whole community. I couldn't let that happen. I can't let all these children down. We'll rise above this, I know we will…We must.

I showered and dressed, knowing I had a job to do after all. There was no time to waste.

'That's more like the Sam, I know,' said Andy, kissing the top of my head when I ventured downstairs. The doorbell rang. 'And it looks like you've got a visitor.'

Helen Jones accompanied by Kelly came into the front room where I was sitting.

'I hope it's OK to call on you, Mrs Jenkins. I wanted you to know that we've collected over £2000 already. We may be a small school but everyone wants to help. Anything we can do, just say. We've also started a collection of books and toys for a makeshift library and play area, too. I said only good quality, mind.'

I beamed across at the young woman who'd been in my very first class when I arrived at the school. She looked after me then just as she was doing now.

'Oh, Helen. I don't know what to say.'

I went and hugged her and we both had tears in our eyes. It was typical of Helen. Instead of dwelling on what had happened, she'd already been proactive, rallying round the other parents for practical help.

'Kelly, show Mrs Jenkins what you've brought for her.'

Kelly had been holding the surprise behind her back and then proudly presented me with a brightly coloured picture.

'I went to my Nana's 'cos the school was closed. She helped me make this for you.'

I looked down at the vibrant reds, oranges and yellows glowing up from the paper and knew straightaway what it was but I wanted to hear it from Kelly.

'Nana told me a story. 'bout the Firebird. I can't 'member the hard word but she said it never dies. Comes out of the ashes after a fire. Then there's a new bird.'

Tears pricked behind my eyelids and I knew I had to get back to work and fight for the school. I owed all the little ones like Kelly that, at least.

'Kelly, it's beautiful. I love the way you've stuck all these foil feathers on the bird's wings.'

'Nana says they're the colours of fire.'

'I know. It's so real. I shall treasure it,' I said. 'And when our school is rebuilt and opens again, I'll frame it and hang it in the entrance hall for everyone to see.'

Andy looked across at me and smiled. Helen took Kelly's hand and grinned at her.

'Oh, we will have a school in the village again. Kelly's made me see that it's a cause worth fighting for,' I said.

My heart raced as I looked out over a sea of young, eager faces stretching out before me. In my mind, I'd gone over and over what I wanted to say because I knew the pupils would be hanging on every word. Staff members were seated along the sides of the large village hall, which was now the Infant and Nursery department's temporary home. Loyal and dedicated, they had worked tirelessly to make this day happen. Bryn Deri Primary was opening after the fire and the school assembly was meant to be a symbol of moving forward, rising up to be an even better school than before. I decided that there could only be one story to start the occasion off. I looked directly at the little girl, seated with her classmates in Year 1, and remembered her visit the day after the fire.

I stepped forward and held up Kelly's Firebird

picture.

'Good morning, children. Today is a very special day when we all start back at school. I want you to remember the beautiful bird in this picture. It looks a little bit like both a peacock and an eagle, doesn't it? It's a very special bird of fire called a Phoenix,' I said, smiling at the hard word that Kelly couldn't remember. 'At the end of his life, it is said he sets fire to his nest and is burnt in the flames, but a new Phoenix is reborn from the same flames. He rises up from the ashes and becomes better and more beautiful than before.'

'This story is called a legend. It doesn't always mean that those things actually happened but legends carry messages for us. What do you think the message is for us here in Bryn Deri?'

Lots of hands went up and I pointed to the row of Year 1s.

'It means our new school is going to be even better than before, Miss. It didn't die in the fire,' said Kelly.

'Yes, Kelly. A school is more than bricks and mortar. This community will see to that.

'Three cheers for the Phoenix and Bryn Deri School!'

The hall reverberated with enthusiastic applause and cheering from every member of the school community. The village school was back in business!

# Moving On

Winter had arrived with a vengeance that year. It was another bleak, December day and it reflected Claire's mood. A solid stone weighed heavy inside her chest. Every morning when she opened her eyes, she felt a black emptiness and even a disappointment that she had woken up at all. A profound dread that she was going to have to make it through the day would envelop her. Since she had returned to live near her hometown a year ago, she had been having more and more of these grey days.

'Why don't you leave my head? You're always in there. Go away! I can't stand it any more,' she said out loud to James. He wouldn't hear. He was almost two hundred miles away. Their acrimonious break up had affected her more than she admitted even to herself. London had been too full of memories and a very lonely place to live once she was on her own. She hauled herself out of bed and made her way downstairs.

What's the point of having a big house like this if I've got no one to share it with? she thought, feeling sorry for herself. Half of the proceeds from the sale of the flat had enabled her to buy a solid black and white semi high above the Bristol Channel. It backed onto a lane lined with trees, leading down a steep path, through the wide open space of parkland and eventually to a grey pebbly beach. She had thought she would be happy living there.

Not long after she had moved in, Claire had got herself a black and white Border collie whom she'd named Smithy.

'That'll help you settle,' her mother had said. 'There's nothing like a dog for company. He won't let you down.'

He was her companion now, but even Smithy's unconditional love was not enough to lift her feeling of utter wretchedness. The only good thing was that Smithy needed exercise, and long walks down to the park and along the beach meant that Claire had to go out of the house.

'Come on, boy. I suppose we'd better face the day.'

Smithy ran around the kitchen in circles and barked in approval.

Claire gasped as she took her first breath of the frosty, clear air and blew onto her mittened hands. At least she was fully awake now. As they made their way down the lane, Smithy seemed to head in the direction of the beach in a very determined manner so different from his usual meandering and sniffing of the plants and trees on the way. In fact, Claire had a job to keep up with him.

'Hey, wait for me, Smithy!' she called. 'We're not on a marathon, you know.'

But Smithy was way out in front. The dog was making for a wooden hut which was set among the trees on the very edge of the park where the grass and beach pebbles met. It was only when she got near that Claire even noticed it. The wood was in dire need of painting and the two steps up to the door were overgrown with weeds and brambles. The only sign of habitation was the curl of grey smoke which emitted from a rusty pipe of a chimney. Smithy began barking at the closed door and Claire realised why as she got closer. She could hear the distinctive playing of a violin coming from inside the hut. Smithy had obviously been able to hear the high notes of the violin almost as soon as they'd started down the lane, but they'd only become clear to her human ears at a much closer distance.

The door opened and a swarthy good-looking young man came out. 'Hey, what's all the fuss about, boy?' he said. 'Don't you like my fiddle playing?' Smithy kept on barking and wagging his tail until Claire had arrived to put him back on his lead.

'I'm sorry if my dog disturbed you.'

The young man's appearance suggested that he had slept rough last night. His hair was dishevelled and his face showed at least one day's growth of dark stubble. Through the door of the hut, she could see the warm glow of embers in a brazier at the far end of the room.

'No worries.' The young man beamed. 'It's good to see another friendly face down here. I'm Barnabus Hopkins but please call me Barney. I'm a travelling musician and I'm staying here for a few weeks.'

'Hi, pleased to meet you, Barney. My name's Claire Thomas. I walk my dog here most days, but haven't seen you down here before. I must say you can't half play that violin. I'm a musician too—I play the flute but not as well as you can play that fiddle.'

'You look frozen, Claire. Do you want to come in and have a warm? Come and tell me all about your flute playing and the kind of music you like.'

Barney opened the door wide and Claire and Smithy entered the wooden hut.

Claire could not believe what she was doing. She had never met the man before but there was something about his warm brown eyes that assured her he was genuine and it was safe to go in. For the first time in months, Claire realised she had forgotten about her troubles. In fact, she hadn't thought about James since she'd left the house, not once. Without realising it, she was soon enjoying what Barney was telling her about his nomadic life. It was so different to her structured life as a solicitor in the City and her life now. She'd never taken any risks. Everything had been planned out, school, university, career. Even her life with James had become so predictable and, she hated to admit it even to herself, boring. But here she was, sitting in this derelict hut listening to a man whom she'd never met before, fascinated and full of admiration for someone who took life as it came.

Barney spent his days down on 'The Island', as the locals called the seaside area, playing his fiddle and busking for any coins that people would give him. The cold winter weather meant that the visitors were few and far between. He would be moving on soon.

'I'd better go and do some work,' he grinned. 'Call in any time you're down, Claire. I could do with some adult company, especially an attractive young lady like yourself.'

Claire found herself blushing. She couldn't believe how much she had enjoyed talking to Barney and knew she would be walking Smithy down to the beach again tomorrow…and the next day.

Every morning before Barney left for his day playing his fiddle on the sea front and every evening after he returned, Claire and Smithy could be found down by the beach where strains of the violin and the flute could be heard complementing each other while Barney and his new friend played traditional folk songs together. Smithy had never had so many walks in his life. It became a ritual that Barney would have the coffee and breakfast ready for the arrival of Claire and Smithy before he left for work and she would have a meal ready for him on his return from busking.

'I've never had company each morning for breakfast like this before,' said Barney, patting Smithy who was wagging his tail in agreement. 'Even better that the company likes making music with me too!'

He winked at Claire. She reddened but beamed back at him. She had lost that grey dullness in her eyes and there was a hint of a spring in her step once again.

She had started to rethink her life. Did she still want to be a solicitor and return to all the demands that the job entailed? She had tasted the freedom of a different life here with Barney. But she couldn't survive without some sort of order in her life surely?

After a few more weeks, Barney told Claire that he would be leaving for Dublin the next weekend. He'd been to the Temple Bar area many times before and he knew that his fiddle playing was always in demand in the pubs there whatever the season. Claire took the news as inevitable but that night was unable to sleep, lying awake until the early hours.

'What shall I do, Smithy?' she said to the canine companion at the foot of her bed. 'Will you think I'm mad if I just up-sticks and move on and follow Barney?'

Smithy opened his eyes, yapped once and went back to sleep.

'I'll take that as a "No, you're not mad" then, shall I?'

Claire laughed.

On their morning walk to the beach the next day, Claire and Smithy almost ran to Barney's hut—she'd made up her mind. She would lock up the house and accompany her fiddler friend to Ireland. She'd start to take risks too, just like Barney. She'd spent the night picturing his face when she told him what she'd planned to do. She couldn't wait to tell him.

When they arrived at the hut, it was locked. She

was too late. Claire rattled the latch and started banging on the door.

'No, no, Barney! You can't leave me and Smithy behind.'

Tears pricked along her eyelids. Smithy started barking with Claire, as if he knew she needed sympathy. The night-time anguish over the biggest decision she'd made in her life was all in vain. She knew then that she wouldn't see her travelling musician again. Life on the road was all that Barnabus Hopkins knew and she reasoned with herself that he wouldn't have wanted the responsibility of taking along someone he'd only just met a few weeks ago. Claire felt sad and a little wistful but was surprised that this feeling of sadness was nothing like the huge black cloud of depression that had been enveloping her for months. She patted Smithy and hugged him.

'Do you know, Smithy? Although Barney's left us, meeting him was good for me. I've learned to take a few risks and not take things too seriously,' she whispered. 'Come on. Let's drag ourselves back up that hill.'

Smithy did his usual trick of running round in circles, chasing his tail and barking until they set off for home. Claire smiled. She looked back at the hut which seemed so desolate and empty now and wondered what might have been if she'd gone to Ireland with Barney. She would never know now.

\*

Barney walked along the deck of the ferry and looked back at the diminishing grey-green shapes he was leaving behind. The sun was just appearing and the ship was almost deserted at that time of the morning.

I wonder if she knows I've gone yet, he thought. A lump formed in his throat. Never before had he found it so hard to leave a place. Never before had he enjoyed the company of another human being quite so much as he had hers.

'I did it for you, Claire,' he said out loud. 'It wouldn't have been the life for you, my love. It may seem exciting now but you'd have soon come to hate it—not knowing where you'll rest your head, not knowing where the next meal will come from, having no home comforts, moving on every few weeks. You could have ended up hating me even.'

Barney breathed out slowly, brushed away a tear and started to play a haunting melody on his beloved violin. But then he'd be back playing down at The Island again next summer, wouldn't he?

*First published in* 'Came as 'Me' Left As 'We'' *(Alfie Dog Fiction 2013)*

# The Journey Home

'Let's go through the lanes,' Fiona said. 'It's been such a stressful week in work. I can't think of anything worse than sitting in a Friday night traffic jam on the motorway. I just want to get to the cottage, light the fire and open that bottle of red you've promised me.'

She looked across at the smiling face of her husband.

'OK, but don't blame me if you start imagining the shapes of the trees are evil spirits about to attack you, then.'

Tom teased her. They always used to go that way but Fiona knew he'd never let her forget the last time they'd taken the 'scenic' route. They'd broken down and had to walk to the nearest farm to phone for help. There was never a mobile signal along this stretch. The full moon bathed the isolated landscape in silver, she remembered, but the deeper they'd gone along the lonely farm lane each silhouette of a tree or a bush seemed to have transformed into a gruesome phantom.

'I did grab on rather tight.' She laughed and made a face at him.

'You're telling me. My arms were back and blue. And you did say "Never again!" Remember?'

Tom turned the car into the single track road. The fading light from the sunset cast an apricot hue inland from the horizon to the hedgerows. Fiona pulled her new cashmere coat around her and breathed a contented sigh. 'The countryside looks as cosy as I feel tonight. I love this time of year.'

Fiona and Tom knew every inch of this road. It had often been their journey home since they'd bought the cottage ten years before. Before they'd broken down, that is. With every mile, they found themselves unwinding and ridding themselves of busy city life more so than when they went by motorway. Fiona dozed, thinking about what their plans were for the weekend.

'What's this up ahead?' she heard Tom say. It was now totally dark and the headlights on the Lexus picked up a lone figure standing by the stone bridge a little way from the road.

'Tom, it's a girl. Stop. What on earth is she doing out at this time? She must be frozen. Look, she's only wearing a dress, no coat.'

Tom stopped the car. They both got out.

'Are you all right, love?' Tom spoke first. 'Can we help you?'

Fiona looked across at the girl who only appeared about fifteen.

'I'm trying to make my way home,' the girl said, shivering. 'I have to see my mum.'

'Here, put this on,' said Fiona, taking off her coat and wrapping it around the girl's skeletal shoulders. As she touched her, she was struck by the fact that not only was the girl waif-like thin but she was extremely cold too. She must have been out for a very long time to get like that, thought Fiona.

'I think we'd better get you home before you catch a death of cold,' Tom said, opening the back door of the car. 'Where's home then?'

'The house is called Broadmead. It's by the Post Office in the next village. Thank you.' The girl's voice was a mere whisper.

'I know the village,' said Tom. 'It's not much out of our way. We'll have you home in no time.'

Fiona saw him look in his rear mirror. She glanced over at the beautiful girl sitting behind him; her face sculpted with high cheek bones and a perfectly formed bow mouth. What struck her most though was the girl's hair. It was fine strands of almost silver blonde. She looks so fragile, ethereal even, she thought. If she was my daughter, there's no way I'd let her out at this time of night.

The girl did not seem to want to talk and any questions Tom and Fiona asked were gently but abruptly evaded with one word answers. Typical sulky teen! Fiona remembered what she'd been like at that age. In the end, the journey continued in silence. Broadmead turned out to be an imposing red-brick house which had most likely been quite grand in its day. But in the headlights, it was now quite shabby and no one would guess that anyone lived there.

'We'll wait until you get inside,' Fiona said.

'No, really. You've been most kind. I've kept you

long enough.' She went to take off Fiona's coat.

'Keep it on, there's a good girl. We'll call for it over the weekend.'

'Well, if you're sure. Good night and thank you.'

Fiona awoke the next morning after a troubled sleep. She'd tossed and turned all night. At first, she dismissed it as having enjoyed the red wine a little too much. But no, something's not right.

'I don't know, Tom. I keep thinking about that girl. There was something very odd about her.'

'Oh, you and your imagination. How much do you bet when we call at the house this morning, she'll be a different girl? Warm, rosy-cheeked, rested after some TLC and her mum's home cooking?'

'We'll see.' Fiona was unconvinced.

Tom parked the car by the village green and he and Fiona made their way to the red-brick house. After what seemed like an age, the door was opened by an elderly woman.

'May I help you?' she said.

'We've come for my coat,' Fiona explained.

'I beg your pardon…?'

'My coat. The camel cashmere one. We lent it to your dau…granddaughter last night when we gave her a lift home.'

'Who are you?' The woman became increasingly agitated. 'I live here on my own. I'm a widow.'

'I'm sorry but we gave a lift to a young girl who said

69

she lived here. Sorry to bother you but I could have sworn...'

'Wait. Young girl you say. What did she look like?'

As Fiona started to describe the beautiful young girl that they'd met in the dark the previous night, the old lady's eyes welled with tears. She turned into the hallway and picked up a photograph from the collection on the telephone table.

'Is this her?'

'Yes, that's her. So you do know her.'

'She's my daughter...but she died over thirty years ago. She actually died on my birthday. An accident it was, just by the stone bridge on the road leading out of the village. We'd had a row and she just stormed off out of the house. It was dark and freezing cold that night. She had no coat...'

The old lady turned her head away, clearly distressed. Fiona looked first at Tom and then onto the hall table which displayed a handful of birthday cards among the photographs.

'Look, I can see you don't know what to think. Come on, I'll get my coat and show you. I haven't been down this week yet,' the old woman said.

Fiona and Tom followed the woman through the village and into the nearby churchyard which backed onto gentle rolling hills that were typical of the area where they'd made their home. As they stepped through the iron swing gate, Fiona felt a calm and sense of peace wash over her. It wasn't long before the old lady stopped in front of a pink marble head stone.

> In Loving Memory Of
> A Dearly Loved Daughter
> Sarah Louise Allen
> Tragically Taken From Us
> Aged 15 Years
> 21st October 1981

'Here she is,' said the woman, kneeling down to pick out a blade of grass which was slightly longer than the others. 'We never had a chance to make it up. All I wanted was time with her so she could forgive me.'

Kneeling to put her arm around the old lady, Fiona said, 'I think she has, don't you? I'm sure last night was a sign.'

The woman nodded, relaxed her shoulders a little and smiled wistfully but didn't look convinced. As they went to walk away from Sarah Louise's grave, Fiona noticed that her new cashmere coat had been neatly folded and placed behind the headstone. Something on top of the coat glinted in the sunlight. She went over to see what it was.

'It's a locket. A gold one by the look of it.' She held it up for the old lady and Tom to see.

The old lady gasped. 'I'd know that locket anywhere. It's been in our family for years. That's what the row was about. My mother had given it to Sarah on her confirmation and she'd only gone and lost it. I was furious with her.'

Fiona smiled at the woman. 'Coming back on your birthday and leaving you the locket is surely Sarah's way of telling you that you can move on now, don't you think?'

Sarah's mother was already fastening the locket around her neck, 'Oh I shall, I shall. This will be my link with Sarah and I'm never going to be parted from it or her again.'

Fiona put on her coat. She and Tom then linked arms and left the smiling elderly lady to spend some time by her daughter's grave reflecting on what had happened.

'I think we've just witnessed the best birthday present ever, don't you, Tom?' Fiona said. 'An eventful journey home, I think.'

*First published by Alfie Dog Fiction (2014)*

# Hats Off To Mike

Mike was due home any minute. Normally, when he'd been away, even for just a few days, Sophie always made a special effort.

'I've got a different kind of welcome for you tonight, all right, Mike,' she said out loud. 'I want some answers.'

She heard the key in the door and he strode in, nearly tripping over a bag of multi-coloured wools she'd left in the middle of the room. She put the beanie hat she was crocheting down on the arm of her chair.

'God, I wish you wouldn't leave your stuff all over the floor, Sophie,' said Mike, dumping his holdall down on the sofa. 'I don't know why you need to make any more hats, anyway. You don't need them now, do you?'

'Charming! And hello, darling, I've missed you too!'

'I texted you to say when I'd be home. I didn't expect this chaos.'

Sophie got up. 'France, eh?' She pushed an open page of The Evening Post under his nose. 'How do you explain this then?'

Mike's face blanched as he stared down at the picture of himself in the local paper.

'I'll read it for you, shall I? Royal Academy painter cautioned after affray inside The Orchard Coffee Bar and Deli. Oh, I didn't know there was an Orchard

Coffee Bar in Paris? It should've read Café Le Verger, perhaps? Oh no, I can see now it's in Swansea—just down the road from here actually!'

'Soph, I can explain. I have been to Paris…look you can check with the hotel where the focus group met…but I got there a bit later than I told you.' Mike looked contrite. 'You know the life-sized painting I did of you five years ago?'

'Ye-es, but how has that got anything to do with this?' she said, her voice rising to a screech and jabbing her finger at the newspaper. Her eyes pricked with tears as she remembered how her thick and glossy her auburn hair had been then, falling down in tresses over her bare white shoulders. She ran her hands through her new elfin-style haircut. Sophie walked away so that Mike wouldn't see.

'Calm down, babe,' said Mike. 'I called into the Orchard to get some snacks to eat on the way to the station and when I was in the queue, I saw these yobs in front of me laughing at a postcard picture of our painting! They were holding it up for everyone to see and were making lewd comments about your…well you know…the bits that are normally covered.'

'Oh my God. Who were they? Do we know them?'

'They must have been some ex-pupils of yours because one of them said It's a wonder she hasn't got her hat on. Miss Allen always wears a hat! They thought that was hysterical and it was then that I lost it. Sorry, Soph,' said Mike, holding out his arms. 'And sorry for being in such a foul mood when I came in, too.'

Sophie needed no persuasion to be comforted in her partner's embrace. 'But why didn't you tell me? To find out like this. I thought you'd been lying to me about going to Paris. My imagination has been running wild. I thought perhaps you were cheating on me…I wouldn't blame you.'

Mike stood back from Sophie. His mouth dropped.

'Oh, Sophie. You know I'm nuts about you. You're beautiful. Why would I ever do that?'

'But I'm not beautiful, am I?'

Mike pulled her back into his arms.

'In my eyes you are. Just as beautiful as you ever were. But you have been a bit over sensitive, shall we say, lately—not that I blame you, mind—haven't you? I didn't know how you'd react so I thought it best not to say anything.'

She pulled herself away, and looked up at his worried face, nodding. Making hats for the charity that had supported her throughout her illness was how she filled her time now that she wasn't working. Giving something back was how she saw it.

'Yes, I have been a nightmare to live with, haven't I? I should've realised that it's been hard on both of us,' she said. 'But I shouldn't have to read this in the local paper…'

'Me and my short fuse. It was all I could do to keep my hands off those scrawny little devils when they started talking about you. Some guy pulled me away. My best work of art and my best girl being ridiculed into a smutty...' His voice trailed off and he clenched his fists. 'I'd do it all again you know.'

She took his hand and unpeeled the fingers kissing each one in turn.

'The trouble is, Mike, it's those scrawny little devils as you call them that I miss most now I'm not teaching.' She smiled as she thought of how they used to tease her about her trademark collection of hats. 'Hats are just not the same as kids, you know.'

'At least they don't answer back,' he said, grinning.

'You know my nickname in school was Hattie, even before all this, don't you?' She had to bite her lip to stop herself laughing as she saw Mike raise his left eyebrow in one of his customary 'are you for real?' kind of looks.

'I told them Some people collect shoes, I collect hats.'

'I don't know why you put up with their cheek,' he said.

Sophie could see that he had been really hurt on her behalf by the kids' comments.

'I like to think of it as banter not cheek,' she explained. 'But I agree they were totally out of order by the sound of it. I'm sorry you felt you had to defend my honour and end up in trouble with the police because of it.'

In school the kids would only go so far and never

crossed that line with her. Meeting her pupils half way meant that they'd really knuckle down to hard work. Those kids would have done anything for her.

It was Mike's way of trying to protect her, she knew that.

'The police were called and luckily, I was let off with a caution. Someone in the queue with me acted as witness. He told them how the lads'd been asking for trouble even before I arrived. Said I was provoked. I'd never have got to Paris for the meeting, otherwise. I missed the one Eurostar connection as it was,' he said.

'Come here. You're forgiven…just don't ever do that to me again, Michael Morgan. At least it's taught me one thing. I can't wait for all this to be over and get straight back to the classroom and try to tame some more youths of today.'

'There's no rush, is there?' said Mike. He paused before continuing. 'I'm looking for a life model for my next painting. Part of my new business venture.'

Sophie looked puzzled and Mike handed her a small portfolio of photographs depicting people with intricate colourful designs all over their bodies.

'I'm venturing into body art. Painting directly onto skin. What do you think?'

'Yes, but how do I fit into all this?'

'I want you to become my model, Sophie. You can help me pick the images, the colours, the shapes and I'd paint you with beautiful designs, naked like before. You could think of it as decorating your scars in beauty and celebrating your survival.'

Sophie folded her arms and sadness rippled through her as her hand brushed her left side. But I'm not a whole person anymore, she thought, no matter how much paint you put on me, Mike.

'I can't, I'm sorry, Mike. I just can't.'

Mike stood with his arm around Sophie as they looked up at the large canvas which took pride of place in his latest exhibition. It depicted a young woman with an Audrey Hepburn hairstyle and large smoky eyes who exuded an air of pride and inner confidence. An intricate design of hydrangeas, freesias and rosebuds interwoven with green foliage adorned where her left breast had once been and contrasted with the alabaster tones of her pale skin.

'I'm so glad you changed your mind, Soph. This is by far the best painting I've ever done.' He smiled and looked around at the large crowd that had turned up for the opening night.

'You've made me feel beautiful, again, Mike. Thank you.' Sophie turned and kissed him. 'And do you know the best bit? Since the painting's been on show, I'm getting so many e-mails and messages from women who've had mastectomies thanking me for showing them that they can face up to their scars, too. Thank you from them, as well.'

# Letters He'd Written, Never Meaning To Send

In the watery winter sun, the cottage looked even more lost and unloved than usual. The once whitewashed walls were streaked with mossy green rivers trickling from overloaded guttering and the paint peeled away from window frames of bare wood. I sat in the car across the road from my childhood home and wondered how things had got as bad as this. If only he'd admitted he needed help. I grasped the steering wheel as I always did, steeling myself to go in. Since Mum had died, every time I visited my father I'd had to prepare myself for the cool reception, the silences, the offhand remarks that hurt so badly. I didn't suppose his precious Rachel got that sort of welcome. And now he'd gone too. I felt tears burning the rims of my eyes. I wished I could hear his voice just one more time. My grip tightened and I willed myself to get out of the car and enter the silent house.

I let myself into the dark hallway and was greeted by a mixture of the floral smell of freshly polished furniture tinged with the pungency of bleach, a trademark of my house-proud sister. Rachel said she'd spring clean the house ready for the family who were going to rent it.

'No, I'll do it, Bec. I know how busy you are. Besides, I don't have a cleaner like you so I'm used to getting my hands dirty.'

Ouch! She'd learned her craft well from Dad. I didn't let her know how the comment had hit home.

'I must do something, Rachel. I've booked time off work, anyway. I can't let you do it all.'

'You could sort and empty the loft, if you like,' my sister had said. 'Perhaps you'd better check with me before throwing anything out, though, Bec. Just in case.'

But she hadn't consulted me when she'd cleared the photos and knick-knacks from the surfaces in the sitting room, had she? I went from spotless room to spotless room and no longer recognised the place as our family home. It was now just a house that contained my parents' furniture. I fought back the tears again as I remembered the clutter of souvenirs my mother had collected or been given over the years of her marriage. Every piece had a story to tell and now each one had gone.

I dragged myself upstairs, armed with a roll of black bags. I lowered the loft ladder and stepped up into musty darkness, fumbling for the light switch. I was confronted with a jumble of discarded items, lamp shades that had been fashionable decades before, old sun-loungers that had seen better days, Rachel's battered doll's pram and even a golf trolley.

'When was the last time you played golf, Dad?' I said aloud but there was no one there to listen.

There were boxes of videos, soft toys and all my

old school exercise books. Where on earth would I start? Dust motes hung in the air, illuminated by the dim light of a bulb precariously fastened to one of the wooden rafters; I began coughing and spluttering and I hadn't even started moving things at that point. I am going to get my manicured hands dirty after all, Rachel, I thought. I decided that, to begin with, I would sort everything by condition, anything worthy of re-using would go into one sack and rubbish in another. Anything I wasn't sure about would be put in an 'Ask Rachel' bag. Why did I feel answerable to my younger sister like that? Didn't I have a mind of my own? I could command the respect of dozens of colleagues at work, chair board meetings for a large company yet my little sister had me doubting my judgement about what was worth keeping from a load of junk! I sighed. I knew that as usual I would keep the peace and say nothing. I could hear my mother's voice saying, 'Why don't you stand up to her? You're too soft. Too soft for your own good, Becky.'

After every session of sorting, I lowered each bag onto the landing and started to see the floor of the loft becoming clearer. I would need help with the bigger items, so I put them to one side. As I moved a box of cookery books from the far corner, I noticed an old biscuit tin that had been pushed behind it. An envelope had been Sellotaped on all four sides to the top of the lid. My father's distinctive handwriting jumped out at me. Rebecca. Dad was the only one who called me by my full name. I was Bec or Becky to everyone else. What could my father have been keeping for me in that old tin? It wasn't as if I hadn't seen him. I knew that wasn't the same as Rachel who could pop in every day but I tried to visit at least once a month. I scanned the attic for another tin with her name on but there wasn't one.

I sat on the floor and lifted the lid, my heart thumping. The tin was full of folded pieces of paper, some tucked in envelopes addressed and ready for posting. It didn't make sense. My mother was the letter writer in the family. When I'd been away at university, her letters were filled with titbits of family gossip, details of village weddings and new babies, and sometimes long-distance advice on how to avoid colds and sore throats. Dear old Mum. I loved the fact that she sometimes wrote sideways or upside down or along the margins to make sure not an inch of space was wasted. But there was never a letter from my father.

One by one, I unfolded the sheets of paper, my hands shaking. My father's beautifully formed cursive handwriting with its even slopes and loops filled each page. It was as if he'd taken such care to form each letter of every word; these were no scribbled notes. I imagined him taking his time, meticulously working out exactly what he wanted to say. Every letter began with '*My dear Rebecca*' and ended with '*Yours sincerely, your ever-loving father.*' They were so formal, no 'Love Dad', no kisses, and typical of a father who didn't know what to say to me. But it was the words he'd written in between the greeting and the signing off that brought me to the edge of tears. They were full of the love and emotion I'd craved from him and I could hear my father talking to me in a way he never did while he was alive. For every milestone in my life, my exam results, my graduation, first job, there were letters of encouragement, congratulations, and pride. He'd even written me a letter when I'd gone on my first holiday with friends to Majorca after my A levels. I thought it was only Mum who'd fussed but I was wrong. *'I shall miss you and shall be counting the days until you return. You know that we trust you to be sensible. I'll say no more. You deserve to have a good time after all your hard work.'* That was a side of my father that I knew nothing about.

Another letter was dated the week after my MA graduation at Cambridge. 'I had no idea what the Vice-Chancellor was saying to you in Latin when you knelt before him but being there in that very special place of learning, I could not have been prouder. My little girl, graduating in the very hall where hundreds of other scholars had graduated before her.' I thought back to how tetchy Dad had seemed when we'd had lunch in the university refectory before the ceremony. For the first time, I wondered if what I had mistaken for indifference was just that he was uncomfortable and didn't want to let me down.

I knew I should be sorting the rest of the stuff and that Rachel would be back soon but I was transfixed, not able to believe what I was reading. I would read just one more, I told myself.

The letter was written after Mum had died. 'I was so proud of what you said about Mum,' he wrote. 'It was right that you were the one to do it and you captured what she meant to all of us. Your words brought me so much comfort and I love you all the more for it.'

Tears streamed down my cheeks. I remembered trying to hold his hand in the funeral service but he'd pulled it away, saying, 'It's all right, girl. I'm fine. Leave me be.' But you weren't fine were you, Dad? I thought. Was it because he was a man of his time that he couldn't say the words he'd written down? If he had, perhaps then I wouldn't have a string of broken relationships behind me. Most of them with men old enough to be… 'Go on, you can say it,' my inner voice told me…old enough to be my father? Was I looking for a father-figure to love me unconditionally? I knew at that moment that I needed to look no further. I'd had one all along. I just didn't know it until then.

It took all my willpower but I placed my tin of letters to one side. I wrapped it in a black bag so that Rachel wouldn't see it and start asking questions. It also meant that I wouldn't be drawn back to it to read more letters. No, I would take it home with me and read the rest there, in private. I resumed sorting the loft. The tension eased from my shoulders and for the first time, I didn't feel guilty about not being there for Dad all the time like Rachel. I had proof that my father was proud of me, proof that he loved me after all. His steely reserve was just part of who he was. I knew then that he would have understood that I'd visited when I could and looked after him when I was there.

By the time I heard Rachel downstairs, I'd finished. I hoped she wouldn't notice I'd been crying. I'd say it was the dust getting in my eyes.

'Bec. How are you getting on? Fancy a cup of tea. I've bought some cakes from the shop.'

'All finished. I'll come down to you now.' She was already on the landing when I descended the ladder.

'Blimey. You've done well. I can see I'll have to re-dust but it can't be helped. I don't think anyone's been up there for years. I went to the top of the ladder once, took one look and couldn't face it. Find anything interesting?' She looked straight at me before going back down to the kitchen.

I followed her and changed the subject back to the cakes. I wouldn't mention my tin from Dad.

'That's really kind, Rachel. The house looked lovely when I came in, by the way.' I'd ask what she'd done with all the photos and ornaments later.

Rachel made two coffees and then came to sit opposite me at the kitchen table. She took the cakes out of the box and placed them on a serving plate.

'Help yourself.'

I looked over at my sister and saw a younger version of our mother, the same fair curls and blue eyes, her busy manner that let you know she was in charge. Her life had followed the same pattern as Mum's too. She had married her first ever boyfriend and they had two boys. I felt my throat tighten. We were just different, that's all. I began to think I'd been hard on her. She was open and said what she thought like Mum used to. No wonder she and Dad were so close. I kept things to myself and didn't share my feelings, something I'd resented my father for doing all these years but I was just the same.

'Thanks. You know you look so much like Mum used to, Rachel, and you're looking after me just like she did too. It's like turning the clock back.' I felt more relaxed in her company after what I'd found out.

'That's what Dad used to say, too.' It was then her turn to let her guard down and her eyes filled with tears. 'I miss him so much, Bec. He wasn't much for conversation, was he? A closed book really, but I know he loved us.'

Surprised that she thought that, too, I nodded. I'd always thought it was just how Dad was with me and I took her hand. I thought about what I'd found upstairs in the loft and wondered whether I should ask if she'd already taken her tin. But hadn't she said that no one else had been up in the loft for years, not properly anyway? I decided to keep it to myself.

'Oh well, I'll just clear up these things and get back. It'll soon be time to pick up the kids,' Rachel said. 'Do you want me to help you down with the heavy stuff before I go? I'll take what I can and the black bags you've already sorted in the boot of the estate. You won't get anything in that flash sporty job of yours.' Back to the old Rachel, I thought. She just had to have another dig! 'You definitely didn't find anything of interest up there?' She paused and her gaze fixed on my eyes, willing them not to look away. 'Like an old tin?'

I knew then that she'd had a tin of letters from Dad, too. I beamed at her.

'I was afraid to say, just in case,' I said.

'I was, too. Why, oh why, couldn't he have told us all that when he was here? Or at least, posted the damned things.'

I held my arms out and Rachel and I held each other like we did when we were little girls.

'Promise me, we'll make a special effort to keep in touch now this place is no longer home. I'll still come down once a month if that's OK. I don't want to stay away from those gorgeous nephews of mine for long. Or you,' I said.

'Of course it is. And I'll come up to you for a girly weekend once in a while—minus the gorgeous nephews,' Rachel said. 'We've got to sort through all Mum and Dad's photos and ornaments soon, too. I can't have our house looking as cluttered like this place used to. Too much dusting for my liking. And promise me one more thing.'

'What's that?'

'You won't hide all your feelings away in an old biscuit tin for the boys to find after your days, will you?' she said.

I laughed but maybe my sister had a point. Perhaps it was time for me to say what I really felt, to be more open about my feelings, and knock down the security wall I'd taken years to build around me.

'I'll leave the rest of the stuff by the back door. If you don't mind, I'll get straight back tonight and try and miss the traffic,' I said.

'Yes, no worries. I'll pick it up tomorrow and give the old place a final once over. The guy's coming to clean the guttering and paint the outside at the weekend and then it's all done. I can hand over the keys to the new tenants.'

We went back upstairs and after a few trips to her car, we kissed each other goodbye.

'Thanks for all your help, Bec. It's sad to see the old place go for rental, I know, but it's not our home now Dad's gone. That's why I stripped it of all the personal stuff before you had to do the final sort. It broke my heart and I wanted to save you from that.'

As I watched my sister drive away, I felt my eyes prick with tears and guilt hammered away inside me. My insecurity about Dad's love for me had coloured my feelings towards Rachel, too. She was still the little girl who had idolised me but she was grown-up enough to protect me from the pain of breaking up our family home. The thought of a long drive home along the motorway to my empty city flat filled me with dread and clutching my precious tin, I shut the door to Dad's house for the final time. I started to sob until I had no more tears left to shed. That chapter of my life was over, I knew that, and it was up to me to keep my promise about staying in touch. I was nobody's daughter anymore but I was somebody's sister.

I sat in the car and texted my sister's mobile.

*'Hi Rachel. Just wanted to say I love you. Tell the boys there'll be no biscuit tin from their Auntie Bec, after all. Xxxx'*

I pressed Send.

# Breaking Beige

Beige-grey concrete faced me through the kitchen window of the basement flat. I glanced up at the narrow ribbon of daylight visible above street level where the sky was leaden, streaked with the pewter of an imminent storm. Solid metal railings edged the pavement like bars on a cage. Yes, my cage, I thought. I wasn't imprisoned in the literal sense but I might as well have been.

'Make sure you slam that door be'ind ya, darlin',' my neighbour called each time I left the house, acting like my prison guard. 'Don't want any of them undesirables getting in 'ere, do we?'

Those undesirables would also get in through unlocked windows so there was never any fresh air in the place. The flat smelt musty and damp. No doubt they were responsible, too, for the obscene graffiti daubed on the walls lining the steep stone steps.

I began to collect discarded empty bottles strewn over the work surfaces and tackled the unwashed dishes in the sink. Better to clear up and get out of the way rather than face another tirade if I was going to escape in time for my secret meeting. He was always at his worst after a heavy night of drinking but last night, he'd gone too far. I looked down at my forearms and felt ashamed. How had things got this bad? This wasn't what he'd promised. Follow your dreams, he'd said. Be a free spirit; go where the moment takes you.

I'd loved him so much then.

'Free spirit. That's a laugh,' I said in a whisper, creeping around trying not to make a sound for fear of waking him.

I took out my phone and re-read Ella's text message.

*'am coming up to london. hope we can meet? u say where + when. luv Ella x'*

This had been the best news I'd had in ages. Ella was my best friend and we told each other everything, or rather, we used to. It was Ella who'd introduced me to Dan when he turned up in our back-of-beyond Cotswold village for the annual music festival. He was good-looking and attractive, someone Ella had known briefly in university. Over those five days, he became a regular customer at my stall where I sold homemade pastries and cakes. We'd hit it off immediately and he made me feel so special. Once the festival was over, he came down every weekend until I agreed to leave home to be with him in London. It had been hard leaving Dad but I had to spread my wings at some stage, I'd told myself.

I'd answered Ella straightaway.

*'Shall meet you by the Eye at 12. Can't wait to see you. x'*

Friday arrived and I was determined not to let Dan spoil my day. As long as we kept off the subject of my love-life, being with Ella meant I wouldn't have to put on a show. I'd be free to be myself again. I grabbed my coat and bag and tiptoed out through the door.

'Off out somew'ere, darlin'?' A voice boomed across the uncarpeted communal hall, making me jump.

'Ssh!' I placed my index finger on my lips and glared at the older woman. My neighbour was dressed head-to-toe in her trademark beige clothes which looked as grubby as the pale lank hair clinging to her head.

'Charmin'. That bloke of yours, still sleepin' it off, is 'e? I 'eard yer barney last night.'

I didn't answer but made my way across to the front door, my heart racing as I ran up the steps to the street. Last night had been the final straw. I'd tell him tonight. If he didn't stop his drinking and treating me like his skivvy, I'd leave him. But I'd tried before though, hadn't I? When he was sober, he was back to the lovely, charming Dan I fell in love with. The one who'd arranged for me to leave the constraints of rural life behind and told me to follow my ambition to become a pastry chef at one of the top hotels. Only it hadn't worked out that way. There was no swanky London kitchen just the local greasy spoon caff a few streets away. Dad had been right all along.

'London's not what it's cracked up to be, Julia. It's a lonely old place, full of hundreds of people all scurrying nowhere, people too busy to talk to you. And as for that Dan. There's something about…'

I never did hear what my father thought about Dan. 'Bye, Dad. See you soon.'

I hugged my father, picked up my suitcase and left the house with him in mid-sentence. Dan had turned up outside and was beeping the horn of his black BMW. It was so different then. He had a good job in the City and the property we moved into overlooked the Thames. I'd been seduced by his promises of London being the place to be, where life was unshackled and easy to follow your dreams, where we could be free to fly to the tops of our respective trees. The colours of cosmopolitan life had soon dulled, though. But he couldn't help getting made redundant, could he, and how was he to know that his friend who owned the apartment was coming back early from her placement in America?

It began to rain. My own tears threatened to fall, too, as I hurried along to the Tube station, weaving in and out of the crowds, people with heads tilting downwards, blank expressions on their faces, mouths in taut lines. I caught the train to Waterloo and scanned the underground map opposite, counting down the stations until it was my stop. Passengers around me made no eye-contact, trapped with their thoughts in private worlds. Beige, anonymous people with city pallors, desensitised, not communicating with their fellow human beings. My life was beige and bland, now, too. A wave of homesickness washed over me and I blinked away the tears.

*

I was glad of the five-minute walk in the fresh air. By the time I could see Ella standing by the ticket office for the Eye, I'd composed myself. I was going to be jolly Julia again even if it was for just a few hours.

'Ella,' I said in a loud enough voice for my friend to turn round and beam at me.

'Aaaggh!' Ella let out a squeal and rushed over, giving me the tightest bear hug ever. 'Jules, I'm so pleased to see you. The village just isn't the same without you.'

I forced a smile, determined not to let my guard down. 'You look well.'

Ella's eyes sparkled as she spoke and she brimmed with excitement.

'Tell me all about your life in London, how fantastic it is. How's Dan? Still as gorgeous as ever. Let me look at you.'

She stood back as if seeing me the first time. Her gaze settled on my eyes and she seemed to look right inside. I felt myself reddening, knowing that I couldn't put her off with white lies about how wonderful life was. My insides knotted and my heart raced.

'Oh, he's fine,' I said, trying to sound calm. 'Let's find somewhere to eat and you can tell me all your news.'

Out of the corner of my eye I could feel Ella staring at me as we walked. My cheeks burned and I swallowed hard.

'Are you OK, Jules?' said Ella.

I looked away. The hairs on the back of my neck prickled.

'I'm not sleeping. That's all.'

We chose a coffee shop with an adjoining patisserie and Ella led the way to a table in the window overlooking a terraced area. As soon as we sat down, she hissed at me.

'Right. This is more than lack of kip, Julia. What the hell's going on?'

My jaw dropped. I looked at my friend and tears started to stream down my cheeks.

'I-I-I don't know what you mean. Just a bit homesick. It's seeing you, I expect.'

Ella didn't take her eyes off me.

'I know you, Jules. Something's wrong, really wrong. I'm not going to be fobbed off with some old chestnut about being homesick or tired. Your eyes give it away—they're so sad. Come on, spill.'

I proceeded to tell Ella about how desperate my life in London had become, leaving out the bits about Dan.

'City life's not what I thought it would be, Ella. I feel trapped, caged in. I have to lock myself in and it's not safe to go out on my own at night. I hate my job, I hate where I live, I've no money, no friends…'

Once I started, the silent tears turned to racking sobs. I couldn't stop. Everything that I'd been bottling inside me, the hurt, the loneliness, the wrecked dreams, just flooded out. Ella looked on concerned and patted my arm. I flinched. I pulled down the cuffs of my jacket.

'There's one person you haven't mentioned. The person you left home for? Here have this,' she said, handing me a tissue. 'This isn't just about London, is it? What about you and Dan?'

I knew Ella wouldn't give up. In the end, I had to tell her how Dan had changed, how, little by little, the real me had been worn down to feel the lowest of the low. I could do nothing without his say so and if I did, boy, I'd pay for it. I didn't have the strength or energy to stand up for myself. All had contributed to making me feel trapped in my beige concrete prison.

'There you know it all, now,' I said.

'Oh, Jules! What a control freak. I had no idea.' She grasped my wrist and I flinched again. Puzzled, she rolled back my cuff revealing weals of deep purple and black. Each one earned when I'd said the wrong thing, cooked the wrong meal, refused the rough sex. Ella gasped and I pulled my hand away.

'He did that?' Her eyes widened, pointing at the bruising. 'The monster! Julia, you're coming home on the train with me.'

I began crying again. I'd have liked nothing more than to break out of that beige existence and get my old life back but I dried my eyes, determined to be strong and stay to sort things out. Surely I loved him, didn't I?

Ella stared at me, and raised her hand to her

mouth.

'That's not what I think it is, is it?' she said pointing at my face.

'What?'

'That mark just under your eye.'

I realised she referred to the bruise where Dan's hand had slapped me so hard that I'd fallen against the wall, alerting our beige neighbour to the row the previous evening. I'd spent so long trying to disguise it with thick beige concealer yet it had been washed away by my tears in an instant.

Dan's sullen face invaded my thoughts. He wouldn't change, I knew that, and that it wasn't my fault as he'd told me over and over. Ella was right. I had to leave. I would leave.


I looked out of the carriage window on my journey out of London. The nondescript beige of row upon row of city streets was replaced by a vibrant patchwork of English countryside. Rain was lashing down outside, making the greens more intense, the golds more beautiful. The view matched my mood as it lightened with every passing mile. The knots in my stomach unravelled for the first time in months. No more looking out at beige concrete, no more peering up through railings, no more locking myself in.

'You OK?' said Ella, smiling. 'I phoned your dad to tell him to expect you.'

I nodded. Hearing the mention of Dad, I

rummaged in my bag and felt for the photo I'd grabbed from the bedside table earlier that day. It was one of him and Mum on their wedding day, my treasured possession. Perhaps, subconsciously, I knew I wouldn't be returning when I left that morning. Meeting up with Ella had made me see sense. I was regaining my freedom and going home.

# Meet Me By The Jacaranda Tree

'Meet me by the Jacaranda tree in the Jardim Municipal,' his message had said. How dare he? He was still treating me as if he owned me, same old Rob. How did he find out where I'd gone? So much for swearing all our friends to secrecy.

I'd had to get away, hoped that sunshine and the beauty of the island would lighten the solid stone in my chest since I found out. I'd been so stupid, hadn't I? The signs had all been there, and I'd missed what was staring me in the face. The working late, the snatched mobile phone after the telltale text pings, the meetings that took weekends away. Why hadn't I seen what was under my nose? Perhaps I hadn't wanted to see. So why would he want to meet me now? I thought I'd made myself clear. Yet he'd followed me almost 1500 miles to meet by a Jacaranda tree.

It's noon when I cross the garden. I'm drawn to the block of colour contrasting with the other trees which are edging the grass. As I get nearer, I drink in the sight of the Jacaranda tree; the beauty of it. The show, the shape, this explosion of flora grabs my attention and enthrals me. It is the first one I have seen apart from those in photographs or in films. As soon as I'd told friends that I was going to Madeira in May, they'd all said, 'You'll love the Jacaranda trees'. They were not wrong. It glows like a jewel, an amethyst shot with shadows of sapphires and highlights of aquamarines gleaming in a cloudless sky. It's reminiscent of the lilac trees and lavender bushes of home yet it displays more intensity and vibrancy so typical of a climate that has warmth and humidity. It's as if all my senses are sated at once.

My pace quickens and soon I'm close enough to touch the velvet of the trumpet shaped flowers. They're hanging like clusters of pyramids that are growing at the tips of the branches. Some of the petals have already fallen to the ground and resemble paper tissues sodden in the moisture of the shade, forming a carpet of softness covering the earth. Bringing my face near the stamens which are dusted in pollen, I can smell a hint of almonds and marzipan and memories of Christmas and birthdays wash over me.

I ask myself why I've agreed to this.

'What are you going to say to me, Rob?' I voice my thoughts aloud. 'We've said all there is to say.'

But, knowing Rob, he won't give up until he finds me so I might as well get this over with. Yes, I'm doing the right thing.

The girl, his latest PA, had looked startled. She wasn't able to make eye-contact as she pulled the sheets—*my* sheets—over her bare breasts.

'Jo, what are you doing back here at this time?' he had said, in disbelief. His face blanched. 'I thought you had a meeting in Oxford today.'

'Well, you thought wrong,' I said in a glass-breaking scream. 'Get out, get out, get out!' I steadied myself by holding on to the door handle.

If I hadn't been so angry, the sight of my husband and that female half his age fumbling and flustering to get dressed would have been bordering on comical. But it wasn't comical, was it? They'd gone quickly in the end, leaving me alone and angry. I don't know how long I sat on the edge of the bed. I lost track of time but it was dark, the room lit only by the lights from the street below when I realised I was both cold and hungry.

The Jacaranda tree brings me back to the present, a miracle of nature which has gone some way to lighten my mood. It has put me back in touch with my feelings after the last few weeks when they had been dulled and deadened. When I entered the garden that day, I hadn't known if I would meet him again. Did he think that by asking me to meet by this beautiful Jacaranda tree I would be more prepared to listen to what he had to say? I still don't know what I'm going to say to him. I must steel myself to be strong.

I can see him walking towards me along the wide cobbled path, the person I had loved so much. Do I mean to use the past tense? The old familiar feelings flood back as he comes near enough for me to focus on his handsome face—those ice blue eyes that twinkle when he teases me, the chiselled jaw, the high cheek bones—and I remember why I'd fallen for him all those years before. I know then that I still love him.

He had come back home the following day.

'I just want to talk, to explain,' he had said.

'There's nothing to explain,' I told him. 'I find you in bed with some dim young thing from the office and you want to explain! How dare you...?' My voice trailed off. I took a deep breath, 'It's over.'

He packed some overnight things and left, saying he was going to give me space to think. I didn't need space, I told him. I didn't need time to think. He'd rung the flat daily, saying how sorry he was, how he'd never stray again. If only I could have believed him. How many times had I done just that?

London had been such a lonely place afterwards. I remembered all the good times we'd had—when we'd first met, when we'd done up the flat together and made it home, when we'd laughed together until we cried over silly things. A host of happy memories, yes, but those had all been scarred by that final betrayal. It had been then when I was completely alone that I decided to get away from it all.

'Jo, darling,' he says, beaming. 'I'm so glad you came.'

His expression changes, unsure of his next move. I stand fixed to the spot, shaded by the tree, instead of rushing to embrace him as I usually do after an argument.

'Did you ever doubt that I would?' I say, sharply. 'Don't I always come back to try again?'

The touch of uncharacteristic sarcasm seems to unnerve him for a moment. But he smiles again and comes close, pulling me towards him. He nestles his head into mine. The smell of the aftershave we'd chosen together, the gentle touch, the protective warmth of his arms are all fighting with what my head is telling me.

'But not this time, Rob,' I say. 'You've hurt me too much. How can I trust you? I took you back last time and you promised...' Did I really say that? I ask myself.

'Jo, you have to believe me. I wouldn't have followed you all this way if I didn't mean it. You are the only one...I know that now.' He looks so vulnerable—just like the Rob I fell in love with. But I grip my palms tight; I'm determined I won't let my guard down. I have to see this through...Don't I?

'I've heard it all before, Rob. You'll never change. I know that now.' I look up at the beauty of the tree that is surrounding me. By asking to meet me by the Jacaranda tree, Rob has actually done me a favour and helped me to stay strong. I know at that very moment that I am back in touch with my senses at last. Even without him, I can still feel deeply and will even love again perhaps. I know I'm doing the right thing by letting him go. I'm moving on.

'Bye, Rob,' I say. I turn, walk into the warm

sunshine and do not allow myself a backward glance, but in my mind all I see is the Jacaranda tree, strong and beautiful against the sky.

*First published by Alfie Dog Fiction (2014)*

# The Bag Lady

Watching her from the doorway of the communal sitting room, a wave of sadness washed over me. My lovely mum, who'd always lived life to the full, my best friend, was sitting hunched and awkward in an upright winged chair staring into nowhere. I took a deep breath and painted on a smile.

'Hello, Mum.'

I sat down and took her hand. The skin felt papery. It was translucent, mapped with raised blue-grey veins weaving their way between dark brown age spots.

She looked confused and pulled her hand away. I tried again.

'Mum? It's me, Kathy.'

My skin prickled and a knot formed in my stomach. It was the day I'd been dreading. Her eyes were still the deep lavender blue inherited by all the Morgan women, bar me, but the sparkle had gone.

'Who?' she said.

'Kathy, your daughter.'

My eyes burned with tears. I changed the subject to the weather. Mum always liked to talk about the weather. I turned away and dabbed my eyes with the tissue I'd been clenching in my hand.

'You've found a lovely sunny spot, here. You're in the best place, I think. It's raining outside, look.'

'Yes,' she said. 'The devil's beating his wife.'

My mouth gaped open. 'That's a strange thing to

say.'

'If it's raining the same time as the sun is shining, the devil's beating his wife!'

Mum's face broke into a smile and for a second, the crinkly creases I hadn't seen for a long time appeared at the corners of her eyes.

She stared at me. 'You're Maria, aren't you? Marco's sister. Same lovely brown eyes. He used to love my sayings about the weather.'

I had no idea who Marco and Maria were. I sat for a while watching the other residents. In the end, I knew I had to get out of there. Willing my tears to stay under control, I stood up and kissed my mother's cheek.

'Bye, Mum. See you soon.'

Two empty lifeless pools stared back at me. Once outside, I began to sob.

'Are you all right, Kathy, love? Whatever's happened?' said Jane Lewis, the manager of the nursing home.

'It's Mum. She doesn't know who I am,' I said, blowing my nose. 'I've lost her.'

'Come on into the office.' Jane's soft comforting voice made me feel I wasn't alone. 'Violet's always happier after you've been, you know.'

'Even if she doesn't recognise me? She thought I was someone called Maria today. A sister for Marco…whoever he is.'

'Yes, even if she doesn't remember who you are.

She'll know somebody very kind has been to see her. You know the photo of you when you were a little girl that's in her room? She loves to tell me about that. She can remember all about what life was like then. I wonder…It's only an idea, mind, but what if this Maria and Marco are further back in her memory than your photo?'

'What do you suggest?'

Jane took my hand. 'Why don't you try to find things from when she was a young woman? Photos are always good, letters, diaries, souvenirs, that sort of thing. Anything to trigger early memories. Worth a try?'

I lowered the loft ladder and stepped up into musty darkness, fumbling for the light switch. Dust motes hung in the air, illuminated by the dim light. As I moved a box of cookery books, I noticed an old leather bag that had been pushed behind it. I sat on the attic floor and looked inside. Underneath the flap was written Per la mia Violetta, 1946, the year before I was born. Could this hold clues to my mother's early life and unlock her memories?

'Hello, Mum.' I sat down next to her. 'I've got something for you.'

I handed her the soft leather bag and waited for a reaction. Nothing. She stared first at the bag and then at me, before handing it back. I left it for a while and talked about the rain that was beating down outside.

I tried again and placed the handbag on her lap. She picked it up and a smile rippled across her face, reaching her eyes where crinkles appeared at each corner. She stroked the supple leather and then placed her hand under the flap that was punched in a delicate open work as fine as lace.

'He made this just for me.' Opening up the bag, she pointed to the handwritten message. 'He always called me "Violetta".'

'Who did, Violet?' Jane Lewis had joined us. 'My, what a beautiful bag!'

'Marco. My first love. A PoW from Sicily. He was so handsome. Black, wavy hair and eyes the colour of melted chocolate.'

She touched her hair and the faintest of blushes appeared on both cheeks.

Jane and I exchanged glances. It had been a long time since I'd seen Mum so animated. She began to take out the items that were inside, one by one.

'I never went anywhere without this,' she said, suspending an oval silver locket from her fingers. 'Can you open it for me?'

My mother may have been transported back in time but her gnarled fingers that gave her so much pain were unable to click open the two halves of the precious necklace. I ran my nail along the rim. Inside was a lock of black hair.

'He had a lock of my hair, too. We used to meet in

secret. Had to. Daren't let Father know. He thought the Italians were as bad as the Germans. We used to meet at the deserted shepherd's hut.'

She fussed with her hair again and her cheeks reddened.

She took out a bundle of letters from the bag and when I left her that afternoon in her private world, she was back with Marco. The look of happiness on Mum's face convinced me Jane Lewis had been right with her advice.


'Hello, Kathy. What a change in Violet!' Jane Lewis greeted me on my next visit to see Mum. 'The other residents have renamed her as the Bag Lady. She doesn't go anywhere without Marco's exquisite bag. Even sleeps with it under her pillow the night staff say.'

I smiled. Mum may have lost all her short term memory but it was good to hear that she communicated with everyone through what had happened all those years ago. I was just sad not to be part of it.

Jane and I stood by the door of the communal lounge. Instead of looking lost, she was taking out photographs from the bag and laying them out on the coffee table in front of her.

'Look who's here, Violet,' said Jane. 'Kathy's come to see you. Your daughter.'

'Oh, hello, Maria, dear. Have I shown you Marco's

bag? Come and have a look at these photographs.'

I looked at Jane and she shook her head. Mum picked up a sepia photograph of a large family group.

'Here you are with your brothers. Now remind me who they are again. Have I shown you the bag that Marco made for me?'

I wasn't listening. I was transfixed by the only female in the photograph. It was like looking at a mirror image of me as a young woman. For the first time in my life, there was someone who had the same shaped face as me, the same dark hair I used to have. No wonder my mother called me Maria if that was her name.

'Like peas in a pod,' said Mum. 'Have I shown you Marco's bag?'

'How's the Bag Lady today?' One of the residents came to sit by us and Mum showed her the photograph. The old lady stared at the photo, looked at me and then gazed down on the photo again. 'There's no doubting which side of the family you take after, dear.'

Before I could answer her, she went back to her seat.

I looked at the other photographs from the bag. Photos of a happy young couple so obviously in love and a portrait of a strikingly handsome young man. A flush crept along my neck and my heart thumped in my chest. Thoughts and possibilities crowded my mind. It all made sense. My olive skin, my glossy black hair and brown eyes, that feeling of being different.

'I'll go now, then. I'll leave you to read your letters in private. Are they all from Marco?'

'Most of them, dear. Bye, Maria. Have I shown you Marco's bag?'

She tilted her cheek to receive my good-bye kiss, sat back in her chair and began to read the faded blue sheets. Marco's bag was tucked down the side of the chair beside her, full of memories, full of secrets.

From then on, Mum's secret would be my secret. She was at last content. For how long I didn't know but I'd have to be happy being Maria so that she could spend time with her first love, her Marco.

# About The Author

Jan Baynham lives in Cardiff. Her short stories and flash fiction pieces appear in anthologies and online. *Smashing the Mask and Other Stories* is her first collection.

Concentrating more on novel writing now, she has recently signed a contract with Ruby Fiction for three mother/daughter sagas. Set mainly in Greece, the first, *Whispering Olive Trees* will be published early in 2020.

Jan is currently a member of the Romantic Novelists' Association's (RNA) New Writer Scheme and a joint organiser of her local RNA Chapter. She writes a regular blog where she traces her writing journey and where she supports other authors through guest interviews: **www.janbaynham.blogspot.co.uk**

She may also be followed on Twitter @JanBayLit and on her Jan Baynham Writer Facebook page.

# Acknowledgements

Thanks are due to my writing friends, Helen Becket and Val Morris, who have seen early drafts of all the stories contained in the anthology. We met in Lynne Barrett-Lee's short story course 'Telling Tales' and have continued to meet every few weeks since then.

I am grateful, too, to Ros Kind at Alfie Dog Fiction for publishing several of my stories, including a couple she selected for anthologies, and giving me much needed confidence when I started writing.

Special thanks to Polly Stretton and everyone at Black Pear Press for publishing this themed selection of my stories. I have enjoyed working with you.

Lastly, thanks to Alan for his support and always being there for me.